THE PORTABLE VIRGIN

Anne Enright was born in Dublin, where she now lives and works. She has published one collection of stories, *The Portable Virgin*, which won the Rooney Prize, and four novels, *The Wig My Father Wore*, *What Are You Like?*, *The Pleasure of Eliza Lynch* and *The Gathering*, winner of the 2007 Man Booker Prize.

ALSO BY ANNE ENRIGHT

Fiction

The Portable Virgin

The Wig My Father Wore

What Are You Like?

The Pleasure of Eliza Lynch

The Gathering

Non-Fiction

Making Babies

ANNE ENRIGHT

The Portable Virgin

VINTAGE BOOKS
London

Published by Vintage 2007

3 4 7 9 10 8 6 4 2

First published in Great Britain by Secker & Warburg in 1991

Vintage
Random House, 20 Vauxhall Bridge Road,
London SW1V 2SA

www.vintage-books.co.uk

Addresses for companies within The Random House Group Limited can be found at: www.randomhouse.co.uk/offices.htm

The Random House Group Limited Reg. No. 954009

A CIP catalogue record for this book is available from the British Library

ISBN 9780099437390

The Random House Group Limited makes every effort to ensure that the papers used in its books are made from trees that have been legally sourced from well-managed and credibly certified forests. Our paper procurement policy can be found at: www.rbooks.co.uk/environment

Printed and bound in Great Britain by
CPI Cox & Wyman, Reading, RG1 8EX

CONTENTS

ACKNOWLEDGEMENTS

'Luck be a Lady' first appeared
in the 'Summer Fiction' series
in the *Irish Times*, July 1990;
'The Portable Virgin' was first published
in *Revenge* (Virago, 1990),
edited by Kate Saunders.

Thanks to Mary and Bernard Loughlin,
the Tyrone Guthrie Centre,
Annaghmakerrig, where some
of this collection was written.

SPECIAL THANKS TO
MARTINA, ALEX, AND D.B.K.

(She Owns) Every Thing

Cathy was often wrong, she found it more interesting. She was wrong about the taste of bananas. She was wrong about the future of the bob. She was wrong about where her life ended up. She loved corners, surprises, changes of light.

Of all the fates that could have been hers (spinster, murderer, savant, saint), she chose to work behind a handbag counter in Dublin and take her holidays in the sun.

For ten years she lived with the gloves and beside the umbrellas, their colours shy and neatly furled. The handbag counter travelled through navy and brown to a classic black. Yellows, reds, and white were to one side and all varieties of plastic were left out on stands, for the customer to steal.

Cathy couldn't tell you what the handbag counter was like. It was hers. It smelt like a leather dream. It was never quite right. Despite the close and intimate spaces of the gloves and the empty generosity of the bags themselves, the discreet mess that was the handbag counter was just beyond her control.

She sold clutch bags for people to hang on to; folded slivers of animal skin that wouldn't hold a box of cigarettes, or money unless it was paper, or a bunch of keys. 'Just a credit card and a condom,' said one young woman to another and Cathy felt the ache of times changing.

She sold the handbag proper, sleek and stiff and surprisingly roomy – the favourite bag, the thoroughbred, with a hard clasp, or a fold-over flap and the smell of her best perfume. She sold sacks to young women, in canvas or in suede, baggy enough to hold a life, a change of underwear, a novel, a deodorant spray.

The women's faces as they made their choice were full of lines going nowhere, tense with the problems of leather, price, vulgarity, colour. Cathy matched blue eyes with a blue trim, a modest mouth with smooth, plum suede. She sold patent to the click of high heels, urged women who had forgotten into neat, swish reticules. Quietly, one customer after another was guided to the inevitable and surprising choice of a bag that was not 'them' but one step beyond who they thought they might be.

Cathy knew what handbags were for. She herself carried everything (which wasn't much) in one pocket, or the other.

She divided her women into two categories: those who could and those who could not.

She had little affection for those who could, they had

no need of her, and they were often mistaken. Their secret was not one of class, although that seemed to help, but one of belief, and like all questions of belief, it involved certain mysteries. How, for example, does one *believe* in navy?

There were also the women who could not. A woman for example, who could NOT wear blue. A woman who could wear a print, but NOT beside her face. A woman who could wear beads but NOT earrings. A woman who had a secret life of shoes too exotic for her, or one who could neither pass a perfume counter nor buy a perfume, unless it was for someone else. A woman who comes home with royal jelly every time she tries to buy a blouse.

A woman who cries in the lingerie department.

A woman who laughs while trying on hats.

A woman who buys two coats of a different colour.

The problem became vicious when they brought their daughters shopping. Cathy could smell these couples from Kitchenware.

Cathy married late and it was hard work. She had to find a man. Once she had found one, she discovered that the city was full of them. She had to talk and laugh and be fond. She had to choose. Did she like big burly men with soft brown eyes? Did she like that blond man with the eyes of pathological blue? What did she think of her own face, its notches and dents?

She went the easy road with a kind teacher from Fairview and a registry office do. She stole him from a coltish young woman with awkward eyes. Cathy would have sold her a tapestry Gladstone bag, one that was 'wrong' but 'worked' all the same.

Sex was a pleasant surprise. It was such a singular activity, it seemed to scatter and gather her at the same time.

Cathy fell in love one day with a loose, rangy woman, who came to her counter and to her smile and seemed to pick her up with the same ease as she did an Argentinian calf-skin shoulder bag in tobacco brown, with woven leather inset panels, pig-skin lining and snap clasp. It was quite a surprise.

The woman, whose eyes were a tired shade of blue, asked Cathy's opinion, and Cathy heard herself say 'DIVE RIGHT IN HONEY, THE WATER'S JUST FINE!' – a phrase she must have picked up from the television set. The woman did not flinch. She said 'Have you got it in black?'

Brown was the colour of the bag. Cathy was disappointed by this betrayal. The weave would just disappear in black, the staining was everything. Cathy said, 'It's worth it in brown, even if it means new shoes. It really is a beautiful bag.' The woman, however, neither bought the brown nor argued for black. She rubbed the leather with the base of her thumb as she laid the bag down. She looked at Cathy. She despaired. She turned her wide, sporting shoulders, her dry, bleached hair, and her nose with the bump in it, gave a small sigh, and walked out of the shop.

Cathy spent the rest of the day thinking, not of her hands, with their large knuckles, but of her breasts, that were widely spaced and looked two ways, one towards the umbrellas, the other at the scarves. She also wondered whether the woman had a necklace of lines hanging from her hips, whether she had ever been touched by a woman, what she might say, what Cathy might say back. Whether her foldings and infoldings were the same as her own or as different as daffodil from narcissus. It was a very lyrical afternoon.

Cathy began to slip. She made mistakes. She sold the wrong bags to the wrong women and her patter died. She waited for another woman to pick up the tobacco-brown bag to see what might happen. She sold indiscriminately. She looked at every woman who came her way and she just didn't know anymore.

She could, of course change her job. She might, for example, work as a hospital maid, in the cardiac ward, which was full of certainties.

Women did not get heart attacks. They would come at visiting time and talk too much or not at all. She could work out who loved simply or in silence. She could spot those who might as well hate. She would look at their bags without judgement, as they placed them on the coverlets, or opened them for tissues. They might even let a tear drip inside.

Cathy emptied out her building-society account and walked up to the hat department with a plastic bag filled with cash. She said, 'Ramona, I want to buy every hat you have.' She did the same at Shoes, although she stipulated size five-and-a-half. She didn't make a fuss when refused. She stuffed the till of her own counter full of notes, called a taxi and hung herself with bags, around her neck and down her arms. All kinds of people looked at her. Then she went to bed for a week, feeling slightly ashamed.

She kept the one fatal bag, the brown calf-skin with a snap clasp. She abused it. She even used it to carry things. She started to sleep around.

Indifference

The young man in the corner was covered in flour. His coat was white, his shoes were white and there was a white paper hat askew on his head. Around his mouth and nose was the red weal of sweating skin where he had worn a mask to keep out the dust. The rest of him was perfectly edible and would turn to dough if he stepped outside in the rain.

They were assessing her as she sat in the corner with a glass of Guinness and an old newspaper that someone had left behind.

'What do you think?' asked the white man.

'I wouldn't go near her with a bag of dicks,' said his companion, who was left-handed – or at least that was the hand that was holding his pint. He had the thin Saturday-matinée face of a villain; of the man who might kidnap the young girl and end up in a duel with Errol Flynn. She saw him swinging out of velvet drapes, up-ending tables and jumping from the chandelier, brandishing, not a sword, but a hessian bag from which come soft gurgles and thin protesting squeaks.

Errol Flynn wounds him badly and is leaning over

his throat ready for the final, ungentlemanly slash when the bag of dicks escapes, rolls down a flight of steps, shuffles over to the beautiful young girl and starts to whine. She unties the knot and sets them free.

'What a peculiar language you speak,' she said mentally, with a half-smile and a nod, as if her own were normal. 'Normal' usually implied American. I am Canadian, she used to say, it may be a very boring country, but who needs history when we have so much weather?

Irish people had no weather at all apart from vague shifts from damp to wet, and they talked history like it was happening down the road. They also sang quite a bit and were depressingly ethnic. They thought her bland.

Of course I am bland, she thought. You too would be bland if you grew up with one gas pump in front of the house and nothing else except a view that stretched over half the world. Landscape made me bland, bears poking in the garbage can stunted my individuality, as did plagues of horseflies, permafrost, wild-fire, and the sun setting like a bomb. So much sky makes ones bewildered – which is the only proper way to be.

She rented a flat in Rathmines where the only black people in the country seemed to reside and the shops stayed open all night. The house was suitably 'old' but the partition walls bothered her, as did the fact that the door from her bedroom into the hall had been taken off its hinges. The open block of the doorframe frightened her as she fell asleep, not because of what might come through it, but because she might drift off the bed and slide through the gap to Godknowswhere. (In the shower she sang 'How are things in Glockamorra?' and 'Come back, Paddy Reilly, to Ballyjamesduff'.)

The white man was beside her asking to look at her paper and he sat down to read.

'Go on, ask her does she want to come,' said the matinée man across the deserted bar.

'Ask her yourself.'

'Where are you from?' said the matinée man picking up their two pints and making the move to her table.

'God that's a great pair of shoes you got on,' he said looking at her quilted moon-boots. 'You didn't get them here.'

'Canada,' she said.

'She can talk!' said the villain. 'I told you she could talk.'

'You can't bring him anywhere,' said the white man, and she decided that she would sleep with him. Why not? It had been a long time since Toronto.

'Would you like a drink?' she asked, and was surprised at the silence that fell.

'I'm skiving off,' said the white man. 'I'm on the hop. Mitching. I'll get the sack.' She still didn't seem to understand. 'Look at me,' he opened up his palms like a saint to show her the thin rolls of paste in the creases. 'I work over there. In the bakery.'

'I guessed that,' she said. 'I could smell the fresh bread.'

*

She wrote this story in a letter to her flatmate in Toronto. It is a story about A Bit of Rough. It includes furious sex in red-brick alleyways. It has poignant moments to do with class distinction and different breeds of selfishness. Unfortunately the man in question is not wearing leather, nor is he smelling like Marlon Brando. He is too thin. His accent is all wrong. He is covered, not with oil and sweat, but with sweat and flour.

The furious sex took him by surprise. She looked at a man sliding down the wall on to his hunkers with his hands over his face. He had lost his paper hat. There was flour down her front congealing in the rain. 'I've never done that before,' he said.

'Well, neither have I.'

'I've never done any of that before.'

'Oh boy.'

'And I've got the sack.' So she brought him home.

'Erections. What a laugh. My ancient Aunt Moragh bounced out of her coffin on the way to the cemetery. I will never forget it. You could almost hear the squawk. It was my cousin Shawn driving the pick-up when the suspension went. Now he was a bit simple – or at least that is, he never talked so you couldn't tell. But he took her dying so hard that he was swinging the wheel with one hand and crying into the other and he drove regardless, with his ass dragging in the dirt. I swear I saw Moragh rise to her feet like she was on hinges, like she was a loose plank in the floor coming up to hit you in the face. And she yelled out "Shawn! You come back here!" I was only six, but I wouldn't deny it, no matter how much they said I was a liar.'

There was a thin white man in her bed, and when he got up to go to the toilet he disappeared through the doorframe like the line of light from a closing door. They were no longer drunk. He stayed, because he didn't know what else to do. He was fragile, like a man let out of prison, who bumps into a stranger on the street and feels a lifetime's friendship. He stared, and she felt all the stories she had inside her looking for him like home.

'So Todd tells me about this woman that he is in love with. I mean that's OK, but why do men have to take all their clothes off before they can tell you about the woman they love? So there we were, sitting in the U of T canteen and I'm saying "Todd, please, it's OK, I'll survive, please put your clothes back on." '

'All the same, I could have spent the rest of my life with him, having bad sex. Honestly. He made love like I was a walrus, something huge and strange. Spent half an hour kind of paddling his hand on my left buttock which must be the least interesting, the most mistaken part of my body. Then sort of dodged in, like I was an alley on the way to school. I didn't know whether he had come, or a picture had slipped on the wall . . . True love.'

He stayed the next day and she didn't go into school. She opened a bottle of good wine to educate him and they forgot to eat. They lifted the sash of the bedroom window and were surprised by the taste of the air. He was so thin it hurt her and his laugh was huge.

'We came across this swimming pool, in the woods, in the middle of nowhere. It was empty, with blue tiles and weeds growing out through the cracks. There was a metal ladder just going nowhere in the corner. So we climbed down and it was like being underwater somehow. Like we swam through the air. Then this crazy guy, he stood on the edge and he said he was going to dive in. My God was I freaked. I could just see his head splitting on the tiles. I screamed until I fell over. Men always think I'm neurotic and I suppose it's true.'

'Are you?'

'I suppose.'

He was grateful for it, whatever it was. Compared to her body, her mind was easy to understand. There were wine stains on the sheets which he wrapped around him like Caesar. He sang, and paced the room, and looked at his naked feet, which weren't ugly anymore. The razor in her bathroom confused him and he asked about other men. So she made love to him at the sink and he looked at his face in the mirror, as if it was blind.

He wasn't so amazed by sex as by people, who did this all the time and never told. Never did anything but laugh in the wrong way. 'They do this night and day,' he said, 'and it doesn't show. Walking down the street and you think they'd look different. You think they'd recognise and smile at each other, like "I know and you know". It's like the secret everyone was in on, except me.'

The light deepened. 'What is it like for a woman?' he asked.

'How should I know?' she said. 'What is it like for a man? Sometimes, after a while, it's like your whole body is crying, like your liver even, is sad. It's more sweet than sore. In here. And here.'

'Where?'

Her touch saturated him to the bone and he had to pull away from her, in case something untold might happen. Which it did.

The next day he rang up the matinée man whose astonishment was audible from the other side of the room. He asked for clothes from his flat and looked at her and laughed as the questions kept pouring out of the phone.

The matinée man's name was Jim and he entered her place with an intense air of apology. Kevin poked his head around the jamb of the open doorframe and asked for his clothes. 'You bollocks.' They all went out for a drink.

What she noticed in the pub were his eyelids, that disappeared when he looked at her, and made him look cruel. She couldn't understand most of what they were saying and they laughed all the time. He was wearing a nylon-mix jumper, cheap denim and bad shoes.

'I thought the friend was the kind of Oh-so-interesting bastard,' said the letter, 'with that glint in his eye that cuts me right up. You know capital P. Primitive, the kind that want to see the blood on the sheet or the bride is a slut. What I mean is . . . Attractive to the Masochistic, which, as we all know, is the street I've been living on even though the rent is so high. What I need is a romantic Irish farmer who is sweet AND a bastard at the same time. So he's looking at us anyway like we've been Sinning or something equally Catholic and I just started to fight him, all the way. He says "Did you have a good time then?" and I said that "Kevin was the best fuck this side of the Atlantic." DUMB! I KNOW THAT! and Kevin laughed and so that was . . . fine. And then I said "Maybe that surprises you?" "Not at all," he says. "That's what they are all saying down Leeson Street," which is their kind of Fuck Alley. And I laughed and said "Hardly," I said, "seeing as he's never done it before . . ." and there was this silence.'

She went to the toilet, and when she came back, his friend was gone.

'Why did you pick me, if it doesn't mean anything? That's what you are saying, isn't it? You're saying I shouldn't have stayed.'

'Don't worry, you're great. You'll make some woman a great lover.'

'You should have fucked Jim. He understands these things. You both understood each other like I was an eejit.'

'I'm sorry,' she said.

He was no longer polite. He walked her back to the flat when he should have gone home.

*

'Welcome to aggressive sex,' she said. 'I enjoyed that.' He had broken her like a match.

'You're all talk.'

After a while he turned to her and felt her body from her shoulders to her hips, passing his hands slowly and with meaning over the skin. She felt herself drifting off the bed through the black space where the door should have been. It seemed to grow in the dark and swallow the room.

'When I was a kid, there was a monumental sculptors in the local graveyard and the polishing shed was covered in marble dust. The table was white, the floor was white, the coke can in the corner was white. There was an old wardrobe up against the wall with the door hanging off, all still and silent like they were made out of stone. And outside was this rock with "Monumental Enquiries" carved into it like a joke. Which just goes to show.'

After he left, she saw the shadow of flour on the carpet, where his clothes had lain, like the outline of a corpse, when the clues are still fresh.

Juggling Oranges

When the play ends, the fading light clings to his body on the stage and pulses gently. His body has been distracting all evening, it moves slowly. He is a good mime, even in speaking parts. His skin looks as though the whiteface has seeped into the pores and will never wash away. In the centre of his face that is blank like a sheet are two human eyes. The only uncomfortable thing about him are his hands, which grow out of his wrists like plants. He is a man to spend your life with.

At the age of nine the world was full of facts, lists and catalogues. There are more pictures than things. He spends the day in school writing down the names of trees in a long row, and sticking dead leaves on sheets of card. The pictures of birds get names as well, but the only one he knows in real life is the single magpie that haunts his mother through the kitchen window.

He does a picture of the sunset in class, because they only have pink and orange paint, and he is bewildered when the teacher sticks it up on the wall.

Billy is easy to love, with his blotting-paper face.

The teacher finds him in the corridor talking to himself in three different voices.

'Are you not in class? What are you talking about?'

'Nothing. It's not me,' and he runs away.

Billy sits in the tall grass with his legs stuck out straight like an infant. There is a beetle on his hand talking to him in a big grouchy voice that wears a suit and a tie.

'Where were you at six o'clock? I was expecting you.'

His father has a video camera and tries to catch him unawares on the beach. Pat pat pat of the spade on the top of the bucket, that is red and has mountains inside. Billy hears the whirr of the camera. PAT PAT PAT. He ignores the eye of the lens, but empties out the sand like Shirley Temple having a good time while her mother is killed in a freak accident. He starts to sing.

He can sing anything from the television and re-enacts entire Tom and Jerry cartoons without a mistake. He whistles songs into milk bottles half-full of water and learns how to talk backwards. He is fluent in Pig Latin and in Morse Code. He makes a set of keys from wood, grass, bottletops, abandoned pieces from his mother's sewing machine. 'This is the key to the chest, this is a secret, this is a key to Jerry's house and I don't know what this one is.'

The girl down the road shows him how to make a bow

and arrow and they shoot raspberry canes over the telephone wires.

Later, Billy talks vaguely to his body in the bath about the state it is in. He lifts his right leg, then the left, out of the water, like a train moving out of a station and he watches the way the hairs all flow one way, and then the other. The dirt of the water reminds him of bubble bath when he was little. Men's bodies look so industrial. When he is on stage he moves like a boy.

Billy tells stories when the mood hits him, never before or after. He sits in silence for large parts of the day and whistles from time to time; *coloratura* snatches with long grace notes that fade into piping conversations between small animals that live in the attic. His stories are long and excited, like a child come home from school. He takes all the parts and has to move around the room. These stories are an expression of love for the listener and they end abruptly, leaving an air of embarrassment.

He has fifteen stories of falling off his bicycle. He closed his eyes on Whitefriar Street at four in the morning and shouted the numbers between one and ten to see how long he could travel blind. If you part his hair you can see the furrow made by the parking meter like a fire-break between the roots. Or he talks to himself and falls off. What were you talking about?

'Nothing. It wasn't me.'

*

If anything, he should be a gardener. On the windowsill in his bedroom is a single morning glory, one seed in one pot. The morning will find him in front of the window, scratching his belly slowly and looking at the speed of it. He has forgotten to dress. Proof positive comes on his birthday when it flowers in a silent trumpet blast.

Billy cuts his hair when the time comes to do so, so that the pictures of his teenage years become hilarious. Even so he recognises the face behind the Status Quo shag as a smell and a laugh, and the sensation of snogging at a disco. He can sense the lights and the girl – and the bewilderment he feels when she smiles like she wants to see him again. When it comes to dancing he plays all the parts and they have to clear a space for his drumming, never mind the guitar.

At college, Billy can stand on his head, or sing in falsetto, do long-multiplication in the supermarket to find out what percentage tax would make South African oranges commercially non-viable. A young man, his shoulders sticking out of a T-shirt with 'Can I help you to find something?' on the front, asks if he needs help.

'No no no not at all,' says Billy and reads the message on the T-shirt to himself, out loud.

Perhaps he drifted into acting. He is certainly not stage-struck, nor is he trying to avoid a job selling advertising space. The stage is where he is eccentric, where he concentrates well. He knows how many people are in the audience without counting the heads. Sometimes, at the end of a long scene, he looks at the faces in the front row and wonders what they are doing there.

Just when he starts to get uncomfortable, he wins a place at a school of movement in Paris. He stays late in the studio and stares at himself in the mirror on the wall, lifting his leg as high as a girl. Slowly, his body separates out from himself and begins to do extraordinary things. His face starts to float. His teachers scream about his hands, which are absent-minded and start up conversations with the audience when the rest of him is elsewhere. He is sleeping with a woman who puts all her masochism into his automatic wrists and requires him to talk her to sleep.

He knows that he will always remember the light in the room and the rumpled sheets that look like a perfume ad. He loves the sound of voices that come up from the alley. Across the way he can see a sweatshop from his window, where twenty Vietnamese women work all the hours that he is awake. On hot days he practises juggling for them stripped to the waist, with five oranges in front of the window, where they can see. He is grateful for their generosity. They throw him a glance and a smile, even though they are shy, even though it is hot and they would like to eat the props. One day he throws an orange over and a window breaks.

This is what Billy means when he says that he is a political actor; a man whose social conscience is eased by playing Wilde, if it is done in the right way. At first he takes any job that is offered, but he is easily embarrassed and hides his performance from the more flamboyant members of the cast. Directors start not to like him, although they can find no complaint.

When he is unemployed for long stretches, Billy starts a one-man show in his kitchen, using the wok and the cooker. By an amazing feat of virtuosity he both mimes cooking and does it at the same time. He juggles red peppers and stirs the pan like a big, hairy witch. The sound-track is made up of snatches of Shakespeare and the 'Gay Byrne Hour'.

'Why should a dog, a horse a rat have life.'

'And it was cancer, lovie, was it.'

'See there, see there, see there.'

'Oh I know, the liver. The liver.'

Billy teaches his daughter how to juggle and how to ride a bike. He buys her a fish tank and she takes the Neons into the bath with her and smothers them in the hot water. She starts to imitate his voice on the radio, in ads for heavy-duty paint, and she dances like a stripper. He bans the television from the house and, on her nights out, the woman he is living with complains hilariously about the amount of time he spends on the toilet. When she leaves, Billy keeps the child.

Billy and his daughter act out her bedtime stories in a co-produced extravaganza that lasts for hours. No one knows what they say to each other. He buys the child a telescope. He teaches her how to make a bow and arrow.

Rose grows older and fatter. The more weight she puts on the more insubstantial she seems and Billy cooks remarkable meals for her, miming all the time. Before he can wake up to her, she is doing exams and is seized with anxiety about what she should do with her life. 'It doesn't make any difference,' says Billy, 'I mean, it doesn't matter,' and he makes her cry. Her attempts at using make-up are a disaster. Billy takes her into the bathroom to show her where to put the eye-liner and the blusher, and realises halfway through the lesson that she is deeply ashamed of him. All that afternoon, he clears out the caches of food that she has secreted, like a hamster, around the house.

He has worked in radio for her sake, and for too long. Over one summer Billy acquires all the props of an ordinary actor, an answering machine, anxiety at parties, various different smiles. He realises that he has been annoyed at himself all his life, and it relieves him to give in at last. It is when he succeeds that he finds that something has broken and his work is bad but popular. He still has the embarrassing ability to move like a boy although his face is middle-aged, and he cheapens the effect. Directors find him useful, they enjoy handling him with little tricks. The audience love him.

He starts to exercise in the front room and recite other people's monologues. When he catches himself singing or talking he cuts it off with a grunt and goes upstairs to sit in the bathroom. His accent sharpens.

Rose moves out of home and lives with her mother while she goes to art college. When Billy sees her at the weekends she is thinner and thinner and her make-up is very pale. Rose is beautiful all of a sudden and very nervous. She discovers a fashionable slimming disease and there are long fights with her mother over the phone.

At the age of forty-nine Billy disgraces himself by falling in love. The girl is a juvenile lead with little experience, hired for her looks and not her talent. She mangles her lines and smiles coyly. Everything about her talks to him about the failure of his profession and he is craven when she walks into the room. The rest of the cast smile indulgently and see that his behaviour is correct. They say that his performances are getting better and better as he shames himself every night for the sake of her smile.

The lights whirr and crack as they heat up. All the traditional smells are there, including greasepaint, though Billy does not find them intoxicating. He puts on his make-up in the dressing room. He looks in the mirror like a blackbird that fights with his reflection in the glass, until the sun goes under a cloud and he sees into the room beyond. The country behind the mirror, Billy used to say to Rose, is the Land Where Fish is King. It was the place where their stories happened.

Ghosts that can not be seen in the room are seen in

the mirror, and vampires are the other way around. Billy wondered who was who on each side of the glass, as he picked at a wandering trace of lipstick, and rehearsed his lines one last time. It would be good to send his reflection out on stage, instead of himself, it was so neatly painted and costumed. But twisting between his eyes and the eyes in the glass was a cord that he did not like, and could not break. In the mirror, everything looked the same, except it could not feel.

He is playing the fop in a restoration comedy, and so carries an orange in a lace handkerchief close to his nose to drive away the smell of disease.

He stands in the wings and watches the end of the first scene, just before his cue. The girl is out there, with an enchanting *décolletage* – too rich and heavy for real life. The lights crack and fade. There is a slight pulse in his eye as he looks at her, as though the light is reluctant to let her go. Her stillness suddenly becomes an artifice, a representation of stillness. The audience clap and she sweeps past him, breathing through her nose.

Perhaps it was the sight of her cleavage, which looked so crass off-stage. Perhaps it was the smell of the orange. Billy walks on in the blackness, looks down at his carefully rumpled hose and points an elegant toe. The light comes up. He starts to speak.

The audience is distressed. There are whispered conferences in the wings. The girl makes her entrance again and Billy's hands go on playing the part as his voice withers away. The orange, the handkerchief and his fob watch circle around him at speed. The young actress panics and skips to her next line then smiles sweetly and goes rigid. One of the older players blasts on to the stage with the book in her hand and a 'is there a doctor in the house?' expression on her face. Billy knows his lines. He knows his lines backwards and so he ignores them both. He knows his lines so well that he whistles them as he juggles, just for her.

It is hard to believe that the hair on his legs is iron grey – one of the surprises of age. He steps out of the bath and sees himself in the mirror. His body looks like it has been pulled out of the canal with a grappling hook, but at least it is his own. He whistles as he dries himself and talks to his belly, then he forgets to dress and waters the vine that creeps over the bathroom wall.

Rose comes over once a week and he mimes cooking a perfect dinner for her – and cooks it at the same time. He says to her 'Now where else would you get tomatoes like that?' and she agrees. He says, 'I grow a very Platonic tomato. It is both the ideal tomato and the real rolled into one. The miracle is that you can eat it at all.'

'No wonder,' says Rose, 'I went off food.'

'You were as fat as a fool when you left me,' says Billy. 'You were a little troll.'

Rose worries about him talking to the plants even though it is one of the things he does that she loves most. Every couple of months she trims his hair, sits him in an old vinyl chair and wraps a bib around the back of his neck. He tells her the story about the scar on his scalp, how he closed his eyes cycling down Whitefriar Street and counted to ten. She uses a small hand-mirror to show him the back of his head until he plants it in the garden in a scheme to scare away birds. When she leaves the house, she finds that a hair has stuck in the back of her throat. It is barely there and it doesn't shift when she coughs.

Revenge

I work for a firm which manufactures rubber gloves. There are many kinds of protective gloves, from the surgical and veterinary (arm-length) to industrial, gardening and domestic. They have in common a niceness. They all imply revulsion. You might not handle a dead mouse without a pair of rubber gloves, someone else might not handle a baby. I need not tell you that shops in Soho sell nuns' outfits made of rubber, that some grown men long for the rubber under-blanket of their infancies, that rubber might save the human race. Rubber is a morally, as well as a sexually, exciting material. It provides us all with an elastic amnesty, to piss the bed, to pick up dead things, to engage is sexual practices, to not touch whomsoever we please.

I work with and sell an everyday material, I answer everyday questions about expansion ratios, tearing, petrifaction. I moved from market research to quality control. I have snapped more elastic in my day etcetera etcetera.

*

My husband and I are the kind of people who put small ads in the personal columns looking for other couples who may be interested in some discreet fun. This provokes a few everyday questions: How do people *do* that? What do they *say* to each other? What do they *say* to the couples who answer? To which the answers are: Easily. Very little. 'We must see each other again sometime.'

When I was a child it was carpet I loved. I should have made a career in floor-coverings. There was a brown carpet in the dining room with specks of black, that was my parents' pride and joy. 'Watch the carpet!' they would say, and I did. I spent all my time sitting on it, joining up the warm, black dots. Things mean a lot to me.

The stench of molten rubber gives me palpitations. It also gives me eczema and a bad cough. My husband finds the smell anaphrodisiac in the extreme. Not even the products excite him, because after seven years you don't know who you are touching, or not touching, anymore.

My husband is called Malachy and I used to like him a lot. He was unfaithful to me in that casual, 'look, it didn't mean anything' kind of way. I was of course bewildered, because that is how I was brought up. I am supposed to be bewildered. I am supposed to say 'What *is* love anyway? What *is* sex?'

Once the fiction between two people snaps then anything goes, or so they say. But it wasn't my marriage I wanted to save, it was myself. My head, you see, is a balloon on a string, my insides are elastic. I have to keep the tension between what is outside and what is in, if I am not to deflate, or explode.

So it was more than a suburban solution that made me want to be unfaithful *with* my husband, rather than *against* him. It was more than a question of the mortgage. I had my needs too: a need to be held in, to be filled, a need for sensation. I wanted revenge and balance. I wanted an awfulness of my own. Of course it was also suburban. Do you really want to know our sexual grief? How we lose our grip, how we feel obliged to *wear* things, how we are supposed to look as if we mean it.

Malachy and I laugh in bed, that is how we get over the problem of conviction. We laugh at breakfast too, on a good day, and sometimes we laugh again at dinner. Honest enough laughter, I would say, if the two words were in the same language, which I doubt. Here is one of the conversations that led to the ad in the personals:

*

'I think we're still good in bed.' (LAUGH)
'I think we're great in bed.' (LAUGH)
'I think we should advertise.' (LAUGH)

Here is another:

'You know John Jo at work? Well his wife was thirty-one yesterday. I said. "What did you give her for her birthday then?" He said, "I gave her one for every year. Beats blowing out candles." Do you believe that?' (LAUGH)

You may ask when did the joking stop and the moment of truth arrive? As if you didn't know how lonely living with someone can be.

The actual piece of paper with the print on is of very little importance. John Jo composed the ad for a joke during a coffee-break at work. My husband tried to snatch it away from him. There was a chase.

There was a similar chase a week later when Malachy brought the magazine home to me. I shrieked. I rolled it up and belted him over the head. I ran after him with a cup full of water and drenched his shirt. There was a great feeling of relief, followed by some very honest sex. I said, 'I wonder what the letters will say?' I said, 'What kind of couples *do* that kind of thing? What kind of people *answer* ads like that?' I also said 'God how vile!'

Some of the letters had photos attached. 'This is my wife.' Nothing is incomprehensible, when you know that life is sad. I answered one for a joke. I said to Malachy 'Guess who's coming to dinner?'

I started off with mackerel pâté, mackerel being a scavenger fish, and good for the heart. I followed with veal osso buco, for reasons I need not elaborate, and finished with a spiced fig pudding with rum butter. Both the eggs I cracked had double yolks, which I found poignant.

I hoovered everything in sight of course. Our bedroom is stranger-proof. It is the kind of bedroom you could die in and not worry about the undertakers. The carpet is a little more interesting than beige, the spread is an ochre brown, the pattern on the curtains is expensive and unashamed. One wall is mirrored in a sanitary kind of way; with little handles for the wardrobe doors.

'Ding Dong,' said the doorbell. Malachy let them in. I

heard the sound of coats being taken and drinks offered. I took off my apron, paused at the mirror and opened the kitchen door.

Her hair was over-worked, I thought – too much perm and too much gel. Her make-up was shiny, her eyes were small. All her intelligence was in her mouth, which gave an ironic twist as she said Hello. It was a large mouth, sexy and selfish. Malachy was holding out a gin and tonic for her in a useless kind of way.

Her husband was concentrating on the ice in his glass. His suit was a green so dark it looked black – very discreet, I thought, and out of our league, with Malachy in his cheap polo and jeans. I didn't want to look at his face, nor he at mine. In the slight crash of our glances I saw that he was worn before his time.

I think he was an alcoholic. He drank his way through the meal and was polite. There was a feeling that he was pulling back from viciousness. Malachy, on the other hand, was over-familiar. He and the wife laughed at bad jokes and their feet were confused under the table. The husband asked me about my job and I told him about the machine I have for testing rubber squares; how it pulls the rubber four different ways at high speed. I made it sound like a joke, or something. He laughed.

*

I realised in myself a slow, physical excitement, a kind of pornographic panic. It felt like the house was full of balloons pressing gently against the ceiling. I looked at the husband.

'Is this your first time?'

'No,' he said.

'What kind of people *do* this kind of thing?' I asked, because I honestly didn't know.

'Well they usually don't feed us so well, or even at all.' I felt guilty. 'This is much more civilised,' he said. 'A lot of them would be well on before we arrive, I'd say. As a general kind of rule.'

'I'm sorry,' I said, 'I don't really drink.'

'Listen,' he leaned forward. 'I was sitting having a G and T in someone's front room and the wife took Maria upstairs to look at the bloody grouting in the bathroom or something, when this guy comes over to me and I realise about six minutes too late that he plays for bloody Arsenal! If you see what I mean. A very ordinary looking guy.'

'You have to be careful,' he said. 'And his wife was a cracker.'

When I was a child I used to stare at things as though they knew something I did not. I used to put them into my mouth and chew them to find out what it was. I kept three things under my bed at night: a piece of wood, a metal door-handle and a cloth. I sucked them instead of my thumb.

We climbed the stairs after Malachy and the wife, who were laughing. Malachy was away, I couldn't touch him. He had the same look in his eye as when he came home from a hurling match when the right team won.

The husband was talking in a low, constant voice that I couldn't refuse. I remember looking at the carpet, which had once meant so much to me. Everyone seemed to know what they were doing.

I thought that we were all supposed to end up together and perform and watch and all that kind of thing. I was interested in the power it would give me over breakfast, but I wasn't looking forward to the confusion. I find it difficult enough to arrange myself around one set of limbs, which are heavy things. I wouldn't know what to do with three. Maybe we would get over the awkwardness with a laugh or two, but in my heart of hearts I didn't find the idea of being with a naked woman funny. What would we joke about? Would we be expected to do things?

What I really wanted to see was Malachy's infidelity. I

wanted his paunch made public, the look on his face, his bottom in the air. *That* would be funny.

I did not expect to be led down the hall and into the spare room. I did not expect to find myself sitting on my own with an alcoholic and handsome stranger who had a vicious look in his eye. I did not expect to feel anything.

I wanted him to kiss me. He leant over and tried to take off his shoes. He said, 'God I hate that woman. Did you see her? The way she was laughing and all that bloody lip-gloss. Did you see her? She looks like she's made out of plastic. I can't get a hold of her without slipping around in some body lotion that smells like petrol and dead animals.' He had taken his shoes off and was swinging his legs onto the bed. 'She never changes you know.' He was trying to take his trousers off. 'Oh I know she's sexy. I mean, you saw her. She is sexy. She is sexy. She is sexy. I just prefer if somebody else does it. If you don't mind.' I still wanted him to kiss me. There was the sound of laughter from the other room.

I rolled off the wet patch and lay down on the floor with my cheek on the carpet, which was warm and rough and friendly. I should go into floor-coverings.

*

I remember when I wet the bed as a child. First it is warm then it gets cold. I would go into my parents' bedroom, with its smell, and start to cry. My mother gets up. She is half-asleep but she's not cross. She is huge. She strips the bed of the wet sheet and takes off the rubber under-blanket which falls with a thick sound to the floor. She puts a layer of newspaper on the mattress and pulls down the other sheet. She tells me to take off my wet pyjamas. I sleep in the raw between the top sheet and the rough blanket and when I turn over, all the warm newspaper under me makes a noise.

Liking

'I'll tell you what happened now, not an hour past. A young girl was sitting in that seat there I'll tell you who it was in a minute, having a glass after her shopping. And she got up to go. She wasn't out of the place when she let a scream out of her and the bags of shopping dropped to the ground and in she comes to me and "Johnny, Johnny come quick there's something down on the beach." So I went, and right enough there was something on the beach alright, and it looked like an old dog or a sheep, like an old dog or a sheep.'

'He did.'

'Like an old dog or a sheep.'

'How many days is that now?

'He went the twenty-one days. I got an awful shock.'

'He went the twenty-one.'

'He was all blown.'

'He was, of course.'

'I tell you. He had a head on him alright. But no face.'

'He did not.'

'He had his socks on. And the sergeant trying to put him in a bag.'

'Don't tell me now.'

'The sergeant trying to hold on to something.'

'How would you like it, how would you like it, if you were standing talking to a man in a bar in London, as far away from me as you are now? How would you like it, if you said "I'll see you tomorrow so," and he said, "I'll see you, Jim, good luck"? How would you like it if he walked out that door, and got the head taken off him with the clip of a truck?'

'He did. And how would you like it if you saw O'Neill on the beach? Because I've told you something, but I haven't told you the whole truth.'

'Don't tell me now.'

'I won't so.'

'I saw him only a week now before he went, walking down the street, and Oh he looked bad. He looked very bad.'

'He did.'

'He was living where? He was living over on the head.'

'He had a woman sure in the house with him. She wasn't from the same family now, but he was living with her all the same. You know he was in the bed with her one night. You know that. You know he was in the bed with her, and she wasn't having any of that tomfoolery and you know he went into the kitchen and up with a knife and whipped off the whole shooting gallery there in front of her. You know that.'

'He did.'

'The whole shooting works. And that's what I saw.'

'You did.'

'How do you like that?'

'Did you ever see a man with a buck rake through his neck?'

The House of the Architect's Love Story

I used to drink to bring the house down, just because I saw a few cracks in the wall. But Truth is not an earthquake, it is only a crack in the wall and the house might stand for another hundred years.

'Let it come down,' I would say, perhaps a little too loudly. 'Let it come down.' The others knew what I meant alright, but the house stayed still.

I gave all that up. We each have our methods. I am good at interior decoration. I have a gin and tonic before dinner and look at the wallpaper. I am only drunk where it is appropriate. I am only in love where it stays still. This does not mean that I am polite.

Three years ago I hit a nurse in the labour ward, because I had the excuse. I make housewife noises in the dark, to make your skin crawl. I am glad he has given me a child, so I can drown it, to show the fullness of my intent.

I boast, of course.

Of all the different love stories, I chose an architect's love story, with strong columns and calculated lines of stress, a witty doorway and curious steps. In the house of an architect's love story the light is always moving, the air is thick with light. From outside, the house of the architect's love story is a neo-Palladian villa, but inside, there are corners, cellars, attics, toilets, a room full of books with an empty socket in the lamp. There are cubbyholes that smell of wet afternoons. There are vaults, a sacristy, an office with windows set in the floor. There is a sky-blue nursery where the rocking-horse is shaped like a bat and swings from a rail. And in the centre of it all is a bay window where the sun pours in.

It is familiar to us all. At least, it was familiar to me, the first time I walked in, because all my dreams were there, and there were plenty of cracks in the wall.

The first time I didn't sleep with the architect was purely social. We were at a party to celebrate a friend's new extension. There had been connections, before that, of course, we were both part of the same set. If I ever wanted an extension, I would have come to him myself.

I asked him about terracotta tiling and we discussed the word 'grout'. I was annoyed by the faint amusement in his face when I said that white was the only colour for a bathroom sink. 'I am the perfect Architect,' he said, 'I have no personal taste. I only look amused to please my clients, who expect to be in the wrong.' There was a mild regret in his voice for all the cathedrals he should have built and we talked about that for a while.

The second time I didn't sleep with the architect was in my own house. I shouldn't have invited him, but the guilt was very strong. I wanted him to meet my husband and go away quietly, but he spent the time pacing the room, testing the slope of the floor. He knocked on the walls too, to see which were partitions, sniffed slightly in front of my favourite picture and told me the bedroom was a mistake. 'I know what you mean,' I said, and then backed away. I said that I could live in a hole at the side of the road, so long as it was warm. 'Do you ever think of anything,' I asked, 'except dry rot?' We were perfectly at home with one another. Even so, there were many occasions in that first year when we did not make love.

The reasons for this neglect were profound, and not to be confused with an absence of desire. The architect and I had both built our lives with much deliberation. The need to abandon everything, to 'let it come down' had been mislaid long ago. We understood risk too well. We needed it too much. There was also the small matter of my husband and a child.

It is a quiet child with red hair. It is past the boring stage and runs around from room to room, taking up my time. It would be a mistake to say that I loved her. I *am* that child. When she looks at me I feel vicious, the need between us is so complete, and I feel vicious for the world, because it threatens the head that I love. On the other hand, wives that are faithful to their husbands because they are infatuated by their offspring don't make sense to me. One doesn't have sex with one's children.

I am unfaithful with my husband's money – a much more pleasant occupation. My life is awash with plumbers and electricians, and I change all the ashtrays twice a year. I watch women in fitting rooms, the way they stick their lips out and make them ugly when they look into the mirror. I wonder who they are dressing for and I wonder who pays.

My husband earns forty thousand pounds a year and has a company car. This is one of the first things he ever told me. But I fell in love with him anyway.

After I hadn't slept with the architect a few times, I took to riding buses as though they were the subways of New York. I sighed when the air-brakes loosened their sad load, and sat at the front, up-top, where I could drive with no hands. I became addicted to escalators, like a woman in a nervous breakdown. Stairs were for sitting on, with my child in my lap. I joined the local library for that purpose.

These were all things I dreamed about long before I met the architect, which makes this story dishonest in its way. Under excuses for sitting on library steps I could also list: simple fatigue, not winning the lottery, not liking the colour blue. Under excuses for killing babies I could list: not liking babies, not liking myself, or not liking the architect. Take your pick.

I don't mean to sound cold. These are thing I have to say slowly, things I have to pace the room for, testing the slope in the floor. So. The architect is called Paul, if you must know. His parents called him Paul because they were the kind of people who couldn't decide on the right wallpaper. Paul has a mind as big as a house, a heart the size of a door and a dick you could hang your hat on. He never married; being too choosy, too hesitant, too mindful of the importance of things.

I wanted to function in and around his breakfast. I wanted to feel panic and weight. There was the usual thing about his smell, and where I wanted that. (I felt his body hard against me. His eyes opened so slowly, I thought he was in pain. 'Oh Sylvia,' his breath was a whisper, a promise against my skin. The green flame of his eye licked my mouth, my neck, my breast.) But I'm sounding cold again. The architect's smell would have spiralled out from me to fill uncountable cubic feet. I loved him.

Not sleeping with the architect helped my marriage quite a bit. I discovered all kinds of corners in my husband, and little gardens in his head. I was immensely aware of how valuable he was as a human being, the presence he held in a room, the goodness with which he had given me his life, his salary and his company car. I was grateful for the fact that he still kissed for hours, as though the cycle of our sex lives was not complete. (Sex with my architect would have been horribly frank, nothing to say and nothing to hide.)

My husband came in to breakfast one morning, and his hands were shaking. He said 'Look what I have done.' He was holding a letter that he had picked up in the hall. 'I tore it up,' he said. 'It was for you, I'm sorry.' He was very bewildered.

If it was wartime, we could have clung to each other and burnt the furniture, we could have deceived the enemy with underground tunnels and built bombs out of sugar. As it was, I rode the buses and he worked and we loved each other well enough.

The idea of the house grew into our marriage. I don't know who suggested it in the end, but I rang Paul and said 'Aidan wants you to think about some plans. We want to build. Yes at last. Isn't it exciting?' and my voice echoed down the phone.

I needed this house to contain, to live in his love. It would be difficult of course. There would be a lot of meetings with the door ajar, talking about damp-courses. The arguments over where the walls should be would mean too much. I would listen to the architect's big mind and his big heart and look at his shoes. His voice would ache and retract. The green flame of his eye would lick me quite a bit. All the same, I would not fling my life into his life and say that he owed me something (which he did; which he knew), responsibility being impolite these days, even with parents who gave birth and bled and all the rest. Besides, all he owed me was a fuck and whatever that implied. I had not slept with the architect seventeen times, incidentally.

I chose the site, a green field as near to a cliff as I could find – something for the house to jump off. We would take risks. From the front it would look like a cottage, but the back would fall downhill, with returns and surprises inside.

Of course he was good at his job. The place rose like an exhalation. The foundations were dug, the bones set, and a skin of brick grew around the rest. It was wired and plastered and plumbed. Much like myself, the first time I slept with the architect.

It was in the finished house. We were walking the empty shell, making plans to fill it in. I was joking most of the time. There would be no banisters on the stairs. The downstairs toilet, I said, should be in Weimar Brown and Gun Metal Grey, with a huge lever set in the floor for the flush. The bathroom proper would have an inside membrane of glass filled with water and fish. The master bedroom would be a deep electric blue, with 'LOVE' like a neon sign hung over the door. *Trompe-l'œil* for the dining room, even though it was no longer the rage, forests and animals, built out of food. I would coat the study walls with dark brown leather and put a cow grazing on the ceiling.

'It's just a house, Sylvia,' he said. 'Quite a nice house, but a house all the same,' as he led me through the flexible, proportioned spaces that he made for me. It was all as familiar to me as my dreams: the kitchen, where we did not make love, with wires and tubes waiting in the walls; the dining room, where he did not eat me; the reception room where he did not receive me, the bedrooms where he did not bed me.

I should tell you who made the first move and what

was said. I should say how I sat down on the stairs and how his big, hesitant heart cracked under the strain.

So we did it on the first landing and it was frank, comprehensive, *remarkably* exciting and sad. I thought the house might fall down around our ears, but it stayed where it was.

The payment of debts is never happy. All he owed me was a fuck and whatever that implied, which in this case is a child. I loved the architect and the architect loved me. You think that makes a difference.

In my childhood book of saints there were pictures of people standing with ploughshares at their feet, cathedrals in their hands. This is the church that St Catherine built. If I painted myself now there would be a round hazy space where my stomach is, and a cathedral inside. This baby is a gothic masterpiece. I can feel the arches rising up under my ribs, the glorious and complicated space.

I can feel it reaching into the chambers of my heart, and my blood runs to it like children into school. We have the same thoughts.

Historical women killed their children more than we are used to; it was one of the reasons for the welfare state. Killing your child is an 'unnatural act'. As if money were nature and could set it all to rights. Money is not nature. I have plenty of money.

I don't want anything so bland as an abortion.

Killing something inside you is not the same, we do that all the time. Don't be shocked. Perhaps I will love it instead. Perhaps I will never find out what is inside and what is outside and what is mine.

We had Paul over for the celebration dinner in our new house, with its avocado bathroom, the bedroom of bluebell white, the buttercup kitchen, the apple-green dining room, and the blue, blue, blue-for-a-boy nursery, with clouds on the wall. I was a beautiful hostess, dewy with pregnancy, surrounded and filled by the men I love. Aidan is a new man. The house, the child, would have saved our marriage, if it needed saving. 'Let it come down,' I say, but the house is inside my head, as well as around it, and so are the cracks in the wall.

Luck be a Lady

The bingo coach (VZE 26) stopped at the top of the road and Mrs Maguire (no. 18), Mrs Power (no. 9) and Mrs Hanratty (no. 27) climbed on board and took their places with the 33 other women and 0 men who made up the Tuesday run.

'If nothing happens tonight . . .' said Mrs Maguire and the way she looked at Mrs Hanratty made it seem like a question.

'I am crucified,' said Mrs Hanratty, 'by these shoes. I'll never buy plastic again.'

'You didn't,' said Mrs Power, wiping the window with unconcern.

'I know,' said Mrs Hanratty. 'There's something astray in my head. I wouldn't let the kids do it.'

Nothing in her tone of voice betrayed the fact that Mrs Hanratty knew she was the most unpopular woman in the coach. She twisted 1 foot precisely and ground her cigarette into the plastic mica floor.

When Mrs Hanratty was 7 and called Maeve, she had thrown her Clarks solid leather, solid heeled, T-bar straps under a moving car and they had survived intact. The completion of this act of rebellion took place at the age of 55, with fake patent and a heel that made her varicose veins run blue. They pulsed at the back of her knee, disappeared into the fat of her thigh, ebbed past her caesarian scars and trickled into her hardening heart, that sat forgotten behind two large breasts, each the size of her head. She still had beautiful feet.

She kept herself well. Her silver hair was thin and stiff with invisible curlers and there was *diamanté* in her ears. She was the kind of woman who squeezed into fitting rooms with her daughters, to persuade them to buy the cream skirt, even though it would stain. She made her husband laugh once a day, on principle, and her sons were either virgins or had the excuse of a good job.

Maeve Hanratty was generous, modest and witty. Her children succeeded and failed in unassuming proportions and she took the occasional drink. She was an enjoyable woman who regretted the fact that the neighbours (except perhaps, Mrs Power) disliked her so much. 'It will pass,' she said to her husband. 'With a bit of luck, my luck will run out.'

At the age of 54 she had achieved fame in a 5-minute interview on the radio when she tried to dismiss the rumour that she was the luckiest woman in Dublin. 'You'll get me banned from the hall,' she said.

'And is it just the bingo?'

'Just the bingo.'

'No horses?'

'My father did the horses,' she said, 'I wouldn't touch them.'

'And tell me, do you always know?'

'Sure, how could I know?' she lied – and diverted 126,578 people's attention with the 3 liquidisers, 14 coal-scuttles, 7 weekends away, 6,725 paper pounds, and 111 teddy bears that she had won in the last 4 years.

'If you ever want a teddy bear!'

'Maeve . . .' she said, as she put down the phone. 'Oh Maeve.' Mrs Power had run across over the road in her dressing gown and was knocking on the kitchen door and waving through the glass. There was nothing in her face to say that Mrs (Maeve) Hanratty had made a fool of herself, that she had exposed her illness to the world. Somehow no one seemed surprised that she had numbered and remembered all those lovely things. She was supposed to count her blessings.

There were other statistics she could have used, not out of anger, but because she was so ashamed. She could have said 'Do you know something – I have had sexual intercourse 1,332 times my life. Is that a lot? 65% of the occasions took place in the first 8 years of my marriage, and I was pregnant for 48 months out of those 96. Is that a lot? I have been married for 33 years and a bit, that's 12,140 days, which means an average of once every 9.09 days. I stopped at 1,332 for no reason except that I am scared beyond reason of the number 1,333. Perhaps this is sad.' It was not, of course, the kind of thing she told anyone, not even her priest, although she felt a slight sin in all that counting. Mrs Hanratty knew how many seconds she had been alive. That was why she was lucky with numbers.

It was not that they had a colour or a smell, but numbers had a feel like people had when you sense them in a room. Mrs Hanratty thought that if she had been in Auschwitz she would have known who would survive and who would die just by looking at their forearms. It was a gift that hurt and she tried to stop winning teddy bears, but things kept on adding up too well and she was driven out of the house in a sweat to the monotonous comfort of the bingo call and another bloody coal-scuttle.

She was 11th out of the coach, which was nice. The car parked in front had 779 on its number plate. It was going to be a big night.

She played Patience when she was agitated and on Monday afternoons, even if she was not. She wouldn't touch the Tarot. The cards held the memory of wet days by the sea, with sand trapped in the cracks of the table that made them hiss and slide as she laid them down. Their holiday house was an old double-decker bus washed up on the edge of the beach with a concrete block where the wheels should have been and a gas stove waiting to blow up by the driver's seat. They were numberless days with clouds drifting one into the other and a million waves dying on the beach. The children hid in the sea all day or played in the ferns and Jim came up from Dublin for the weekend.

'This is being happy,' she thought, scattering the contents of the night bucket over the scutch grass or trekking to the shop. She started counting the waves in order to get to sleep.

She knew before she realised it. She knew without visitation, without a slant of light cutting into the sea. There was no awakening, no manifestation, no pause in the angle of the stairs. There may have been a smile as she took the clothes pegs out of her mouth and the wind blew the washing towards her, but it was forgotten before it happened. She just played Patience all day on the fold-down table in a derelict bus and watched the cards making sense.

By the age of 55 she had left the cards behind. She found them obvious and untrustworthy – they tried to tell you too much and in the wrong way. The Jack of Spades sat on the Queen of Hearts, the clubs hammered away in a row. Work, love, money, pain; clubs, hearts, diamonds, spades, all making promises too big to keep. The way numbers spoke to her was much more bewildering and ordinary. Even the bingo didn't excite or let her down, it soothed her. It let her know in advance.

5 roses: the same as
5 handshakes at a railway station: the same as
5 women turning to look when a bottle of milk smashes in the shop: the same as
5 children: the same as
5 odd socks in the basket
5 tomatoes on the window-sill

5 times she goes to the toilet before she can get to sleep.
and all different from

4 roses, 4 shakes of the hand, 4 women turning, 4 children, 4 odd socks, 4 tomatoes in the sun, 4 times she goes to the toilet and lies awake thinking about the 5th.

The numbers rushed by her in strings and verification came before the end of any given day. They had a party all around her, talking, splitting, reproducing, sitting by themselves in a corner of the room. She smoked them, she hung them out on the line to dry, they chattered to her out from the TV. They drummed on the table-top and laughed in their intimate, syncopated way. They were music.

She told no one and did the cards for people if they asked. It was very accurate if she was loose enough on the day, but her husband didn't like it. He didn't like the bingo either and who could blame him.

'When's it going to stop?' he would say, or 'the money's fine, I don't mind the money.'

'With a bit of luck,' she said, 'my luck will run out.'

On Wednesday nights she went with Mrs Power to the local pub, because there was no bingo. They sat in the upstairs lounge where the regulars went, away from the people who were too young to be there at all. Mr Finn took the corner stool, Mr Byrne was centre-forward. In the right-hand corner Mr Slevin sat and gave his commentary on the football match that was being played out in his head. The other women sat in their places around the walls. No one let on to be drunk. Pat the barman knew their orders and which team were going to get to the final. At the end of the bar, Pauline made a quiet disgrace of herself, out on her own and chatty.

'His days are numbered . . .' said a voice at the bar, and Mrs Hanratty's listened to her blood quicken. 'That fella's days are *numbered.*' There was a middle-aged man standing to order like a returned Yank in a shabby suit with a fat wallet. He was drunk and proud of it.

'I've seen his kind before,' he counted out the change in his pocket carefully in 10s and 2s and 5s, and the barman scooped all the coins into one mess and scattered them into the till. Mrs Hanratty took more than her usual sip of vodka and orange.

'None of us, of course,' he commented, though the barman had moved to the other end of the counter, 'are exempt.'

It was 2 weeks before he made his way over to their table, parked his drink and would not sit until he was asked. 'I've been all over,' he told them. 'You name it, I've done it. All over,' and he started to sing something about Alaska. It had to be a lie.

'Canada,' he started. 'There's a town in the Rockies called Hope. Just like that. And a more miserable stretch of hamburger joints and shacks you've never seen. Lift your eyes 30 degrees and you have the dawn coming over the mountains and air so thin it makes you feel the world is full of . . . well what? I was going to say "lovely ladies" but look at the two I have at my side.' She could feel Mrs Power's desire to leave as big and physical as a horse standing beside her on the carpet.

He rubbed his thigh with his hand, and, as if reminded slapped the tables with 3 extended fingers. There was no 4th. 'Look at that,' he said, and Mrs Power gave a small whinny. 'There should be a story there about how I lost it, but do you know something? It was the simplest thing in the County Meath where I was as a boy. The simplest thing. A dirty cut and it swelled so bad I was lucky I kept the hand. Isn't that a good one? I worked a combine harvester on the great plains in Iowa and you wouldn't believe the fights I got into as a young fella as far away as . . . Singapore – believe *that* or not. But a dirty cut in the County Meath.' And he wrapped the 3 fingers around his glass and toasted them silently. That night, for the first time in her life, Maeve Hanratty lost count of the vodkas she drank.

She wanted him. It was as simple as that. A woman of 55, a woman with 5 children and 1 husband, who had had sexual intercourse 1,332 times in her life and was in possession of 14 coal-scuttles, wanted the 3-fingered man, because he had 3 fingers and not 4.

It was a commonplace sickness and one she did not indulge. Her daughter came in crying from the dance-hall, her husband (and not her father) spent the bingo money on the horses. The house was full of torn betting slips and the stubs of old lipstick. Mrs Hanratty went to bingo and won and won and won.

Although she had done nothing, she said to him silently, 'Well it's your move now, I'm through with all that,' and for 3 weeks in a row he sat at the end of the bar and talked to Pauline, who laughed too much. 'If that's what he wants, he can have it,' said Mrs Hanratty, who believed in dignity, as well as numbers.

The numbers were letting her down. Her daily walk to the shops became a confusion of damaged registration plates, the digits swung sideways or strokes were lopped off. 6 became o, 7 turned into 1. She added up what was left, 555, 666, 616, 707, 906, 888, the numbers for parting, for grief, for the beginning of grief, forgetting, for accidents and for the hate that comes from money.

On the next Wednesday night he was wide open and roaring. He talked about his luck, that had abandoned him one day in Ottawa when he promised everything to a widow in the timber trade. The whole bar listened and Mrs Hanratty felt their knowledge of her as keen as a son on drugs or the front of the house in a state. He went to the box of plastic plants and ransacked it for violets which were presented to her with a mock bow. How many were there? 3 perhaps, or 4 – but the bunch loosened out before her and all Mrs Hanratty could see were the purple plastic shapes and his smile.

She took to her bed with shame, while a zillion a trillion a billion a million numbers opened up before her and wouldn't be pinned down at 6 or 7 or 8. She felt how fragile the world was with so much in it and confined herself to Primes, that were out on their own except for 1.

'The great thing about bingo is that no one loses,' Mrs Power had told him about their Tuesday and Thursday nights. Mrs Hanratty felt flayed in the corner, listening to him and his pride. Her luck was leaking into the seat as he invited himself along, to keep himself away from the drink, he said. He had nothing else to do.

The number of the coach was NIE 133. Mrs Maguire, Mrs Power and Mrs Hanratty climbed on board and took their places with the 33 women and 1 man who made up this Thursday run. He sat at the back and shouted for them to come and join him, and there was hooting from the gang at the front. He came up the aisle instead and fell into the seat beside Mrs Hanratty with a bend in the road. She was squeezed over double, paddling her hand on the floor in search of 1 ear-ring which she may have lost before she got on at all.

He crossed his arms with great ceremony, and not even the violence with which the coach turned corners could convince Mrs Hanratty that he was not rubbing her hand, strangely, with his 3 fingers, around and around.

'I am a 55-year-old woman who has had sex 1,332 times in my life and I am being molested by a man I should never have spoken to in the first place.' The action of his hand was polite and undemanding and Mrs Hanratty resented beyond anger the assurance of its tone.

All the numbers were broken off the car parked outside the hall, except 0, which was fine – it was the only 1 she knew anymore. Mrs Hanratty felt the justice of it, though it made her feel so lonely. She had betrayed her own mind and her friends were strange to her. Her luck was gone.

The 3-fingered man was last out of the coach and he called her back. 'I have your ear-ring! Maeve!' She listened. She let the others walk through. She turned.

His face was a jumble of numbers as he brought his hand up in mock salute. Out of the mess she took: his 3 fingers; the arching 3 of his eyebrows, which was laughing; the tender 3 of his upper lip and the 1 of his mouth, which opened into 0 as he spoke.

'You thought you'd lost it!' and he dropped the *diamanté* into her hand.

'I thought I had.'

He smiled and the numbers of his face scattered and disappeared. His laughter multiplied out around her like a net.

'So what are you going to win tonight then?'

'Nothing. You.'

'0'

The Portable Virgin

Dare to be dowdy! that's my motto, because it comes to us all – the dirty acrylic jumpers and the genteel trickle of piss down our support tights. It will come to her too.

She was one of those women who hold their skin like a smile, as if she was afraid her face might fall off if the tension went out of her eyes.

I knew that when Ben made love to her, the thought that she might break pushed him harder. I, by comparison, am like an old sofa, welcoming, familiar, well-designed.

This is the usual betrayal story, as you have already guessed – the word 'sofa' gave it away. The word 'sofa' opened up rooms full of sleeping children and old wedding photographs, ironic glances at crystal wine-glasses, BBC mini-series where Judi Dench plays the deserted furniture and has a little sad fun.

*

It is not a story about hand-jobs in toilets, at parties where everyone is in the van-rental business. It is not a story where Satan turns around like a lawyer in a swivel chair. There are no doves, no prostitutes, no railway stations, no marks on the skin. So there I was knitting a bolero jacket when I dropped a stitch. Bother. And there was Ben with a gin and tonic crossing his legs tenderly by the phone.

'Thoroughly fucked?' I asked and he spilt his drink.

Ben has been infected by me over the years. He has my habit of irony, or perhaps I have his. Our inflections coincide in bed, and sometimes he startles me in the shops, by hopping out of my mouth.

'Thoroughly,' he said, brushing the wet on his trousers and flicking drops of gin from his fingertips.

There was an inappropriate desire in the room and a strange dance of description as I uncovered her brittle blonde hair, her wide strained mouth. A woman replete with modified adjectives, damaged by men, her body whittled into thinness so unnatural you could nearly see the marks of the knife. Intelligent? No. Funny? No. Rich, with a big laugh and sharp heels? No. Happy? Definitely not. Except when he was there. Ben makes me too sad for words. I finished the row, put away my needles and went to bed.

*

Judi Dench came out of the wardrobe and decided that it was time that she had an affaire herself. She would start a small business in the gardening shed and leave her twin-sets behind. And just when she realised that *she* was a human being *too* – attractive generous and witty (albeit in a sofa kind of way) – some nice man would come along and agree with her.

Mrs Rochester punched a hole in the ceiling and looked at Ben where he sat at the end of the bed, maimed and blind. She whispered a long and very sensible monologue with an urgency that made the mattress smoulder, and we both had a good laugh about that.

Karen . . . Sharon . . . Teresa . . . all good names for women who dye their hair. Suzy . . . Jacintha . . . Patti . . .

'What's her name?' I asked.
'Mary,' he said.

My poor maimed husband is having sex in the back of our car with a poor maimed woman who has a law degree and a tendency to overdress. She works for a van-rental firm. You would think at least she could get them something with a bigger back seat.

My poor maimed husband is seriously in danger of damaging his health with the fillip this fact has given to our love life. And while he bounces on top of his well-loved sofa, Satan turns around in the corner, like a lawyer in a swivel chair, saying 'Go on, go on, you'll wake the children.' (Or is that me?)

She is the silence at the other end of the phone. She is the smile he starts but does not finish. She is the woman standing at the top of the road, with cheap nail-polish and punctured ears. She is the girl at the front of the class, with ringlets and white knees and red eyes.

The phonecalls are more frequent. It is either getting serious or going sour. He used to head straight for the bathroom when he came home, in order to put his dick in the sink. Then he stopped doing it by accident and started going to her flat instead, with its (naturally) highly scented soap. Should I tell her the next time she rings? Should we get chatty about Pears, fall in love over Palmolive? We could ring up an agency and do an advert, complete with split screen. 'Mary's soap is all whiffy, but *Mary* uses X – so mild her husband will never leave.' Of course we have the same name, it is part of Ben's sense of irony, and we all know where he got that from.

So Ben is tired of love. Ben wants sad sex in the back of cars. Ben wants to desire the broken cunt of a woman who will never make it to being real.

'But I thought it *meant* something!' screams the wife, throwing their crystal honeymoon wineglasses from Seville against the Magnolia Matt wall.

I am not that old after all. Revenge is not out of the question. There is money in my purse and an abandoned adolescence that never got under way.

I sit in a chair in the most expensive hairdresser in Grafton Sreet and a young man I can't see pulls my head back into the sink and anoints (I'm sorry) my head with shampoo. It is interesting to be touched like this; hairdressers, like doctors, are getting younger by the day. My 'stylist' is called Alison and she checks my shoes beneath the blue nylon cape, looking for a clue.

'I want a really neat bob,' I say, 'but I don't know what to do with this bit.'

'I know,' she says, 'it's driving you mad. That's why it's so thin, you just keep brushing it out of your eyes.'

I am a woman whose hair is falling out, my stuffing is coming loose.

'But look, we're nearly there,' and she starts to wave the scissors (like a blessing) over my head.

'How long is it since you had it cut last?'

'About ten weeks.'

'Exactly,' she says, 'because we're not going to get any length with all these split ends, are we?'

'I want to go blonde,' says the wet and naked figure in the mirror and the scissors pause mid-swoop.

'It's very thin . . .'

'I know, I want it to break. I want it blonde.'

'Well . . .' My stylist is shocked. I have finally managed to say something really obscene.

The filthy metamorphosis is effected by another young man whose hair is the same length as the stubble on his chin. He has remarkable, sexual blue eyes, which come with the price. 'We' start with a rubber cap which he punctures with a vicious crochet hook, then drags my poor thin hair through the holes. I look 'a fright'. All the women around me look 'a fright'. Mary is sitting to my left and to my right. She is blue from the neck down, she is reading a magazine, her hair stinks, her skin is pulled into a smile by the rubber tonsure on her head. There is a handbag at her feet, the inside of which is coated with blusher that came loose. Inside the bags are bills, pens, sweet-papers, diaphragms, address books full of people she doesn't know anymore. I know this because I stole one as I left the shop.

I am sitting on Dollymount Strand going through Mary's handbag, using her little mirror, applying her 'Wine Rose and Gentlelight Colourize Powder

Shadow Trio', her Plumsilk lipstick, her Venetian Brocade blusher and her Tearproof (thank God) mascara.

I will be bored soon. I will drown her slowly in a pool and let the police peg out the tatters to dry when they pick up the bag on the beach. It affords me some satisfaction to think of her washed up in the hair-dressers, out of her nylon shift and newly shriven, without the means to pay.

My revenge looks back at me, out of the mirror. The new fake me looks twice as real as the old. Underneath my clothes my breasts have become blind, my iliac crests mottle and bruise. Strung out between my legs is a triangle of air that pulls away from sex, while my hands clutch. It used to be the other way around.

I root through the bag, looking for a past. At the bottom, discoloured by Wine Rose and Gentlelight, I find a small, portable Virgin. She is made of trans-parent plastic, except for her cloak, which is coloured blue. 'A present from Lourdes' is written on the globe at her feet, underneath her heel and the serpent. Mary is full of surprises. Her little blue crown is a screw-off top, and her body is filled with holy water, which I drink.

*

Down by the water's edge I set her sailing on her back, off to Ben, who is sentimental that way. Then I follow her into his story, with its doves and prostitutes, railway stations and marks on the skin. I have nowhere else to go. I love that man.

Science and Nature

I wanted to buy him balloons. His eyes had a clean, pained look, a wide colour. They were always disappointed to find no kites when he looked into the sky.

It was not that he disliked sentiment. He was a sop of sentiment, nostalgic all the time. He just disliked the words that were put on it, the loss of secrecy. Nothing made him aggressive like the loss of a secret.

We were working away at the kitchen counter, chopping carrots, onions and peppers with a precision that made it seem an unusual task. 'You're such a precise person.' He turned as though I had caught him in the act.

'No I'm not,' he said.

He loved graveyards and parks. They 'emptied him out'. There is a feeling of connectedness in a graveyard, like a crossword puzzle that is all filled up. High-rise stacks of bodies along supermarket aisles. Parks, on the other hand, are full of accidents and nostalgia, bumped heads and ice-creams, social mixtures – before everything got too complicated instead of after. All of this, of course, I find suspect, and that is why I brought him to the zoo.

The llama has a hare-lip. It has a nosy, indifferent air and a lip at the end of its face that splits to grab the foliage offered over the ditch. The ant-eater too, has a crippled face and kisses with its nose. The polar bears surprised me by the yellow of their teeth, as though I could smell the bad, meaty breath from behind the wire. I had wanted to concentrate on the primates, and make the trip a moral, or comic, trail, but the polar bears were as insistent as a famine on the nine-o'clock news. We saw them from the other side of the lake, criss-crossing all afternoon, walking backwards, then forwards, then backwards again.

We theorised about the bears. I said that they walk hundreds of miles a day in the wild, and just couldn't stop themselves. He told me of a dentist who claimed it was toothache that made them shake their heads from side to side, as though they were in pain. I countered with the fact that their fur was the natural equivalent of optic fibres: each hair was hollow in the middle to trap the rays of the sun and keep them warm. 'They must be baked alive – carpeted with hot needles.'

In the monkey house, marmosets played with their own dung and remained picturesque. Salient fact number thirty-four, I said, caged animals fight and masturbate, but do not mate.

We had a trivia competition for most useless fact. He started.

'There was a certain line of French nobles who considered it polite to shave themselves from head to toe on the day that they were married in order to spare their new wives the fright.'

'Alright,' I said, 'but what about the Marquis de Champfleury, who was so shocked on his wedding night by the pinkness of his wife's skin, that he ran away. Then he came back when she was asleep, painted her white from head to toe, and jumped on her.'

'The ladies of Versailles used to lift their skirts in the corner of the room and piss.'

'On the contrary,' I said, 'the ladies of Versailles had a special kind of china chamber pot that could be carried under their dresses, and it was called after the court priest because he gave such long sermons.'

The monkeys remained picturesque as he recited the microfiche. 'On the general index,' he told me, 'sex comes between "semiotics" and "social policy".' I laughed. (Is this how undergraduates do it?) 'The actual index reads:

"Sewage disposal
Sex
Shadow prices
Shamanism
Shape discrimination
Sheep
Sheldon High School"'

He won.

Winning always made him sad, which is what attracted me to him in the first place; he never did it conspicuously. His essays were neat and well developed; there was something seductive and clean about them, a melancholy in stating the obvious. It made me curious as hell. All my own tragedies were small and spectacular. They made him retreat into his Secret, whatever it was.

Then on to the reptiles, a lot of depressed snakes in boxes. From Kiddies Korner came the sound of a cow in pain. 'She's in heat,' he said. 'What do the snakes do? Swallow their own tails?' and he rapped on the glass with a bright new penny, shy and precise.

It was a pleasant enough afternoon, apart from attacks of mental asphyxiation in front of one cage or another. His eyes remained clean and wide, as I tried to prise him open with an extremely seductive monologue on the miracle of the sperm whale, complete with literary references. I linked arms with him and talked about oceans, whale song, mating rituals. 'Maybe there is only one left,' I said, 'can you imagine? In the spring it swims the length of the Atlantic, down around South America, and then it swings up through the Pacific, singing all the time. Listening for a reply.' Perhaps I didn't mention the singing.

'No whales in the zoo,' he said, just to annoy, and he checked the sky for kites.

'Let's hide in the bushes and stay the night,' he said. 'Let's see what they do when all the people are gone. They probably watch the moon like we watch the telly. Have a drink, chew the cud, go dancing, make love a bit. A simple life. No one asking questions. No one looking on.'

I was annoyed, 'There are two young polar bears in Belfast Zoo,' I told him, 'that were bred in captivity. Totally shameless. They lie on their sides all day and stroke each other, nothing else.'

'No,' he said, for some reason, and it occured to me that his secret was simple. I was part of it. The Secret was me.

We walked towards the sea-lions' pool. where the whales were making love; with tidal waves and cracks in the concrete. The seals barked and applauded with their flippers while delighted children screamed at the rails, throwing in entire ice-creams.

'I wonder where they bury the animals,' he said.

Men and Angels

The watchmaker and his wife live in a small town in Germany and his eyesight is failing.

He is the inventor of the device which is called after him, namely 'Huygens' Endless Chain', a system that allows the clock to keep ticking while it is being wound. It is not perfect, it does not work if the clock is striking. Even so Huygens is proud of his invention because in clocks all over Europe there is one small part that bears his name.

Two pulleys are looped by a continuous chain, on which are hung a large and a small weight. The clock is wound by pulling on the small weight, which causes the large weight to rise. Over the hours, the slow pull of its descent makes the clock tick.

The small weight is sometimes replaced by a ring, after the fact that when Huygens was building the original model, his impatience caused him to borrow his wife's wedding ring to hang on the chain. The ring provided a perfect balance, and Huygens left it where it was. He placed the whole mechanism under a glass bell and put it on the mantelpiece, where his wife could see the ring slowly rise with the passing of the hours, and fall again when the clock was wound.

Despite the poetry of the ring's motion, and despite the patent which kept them all in food and clothes, Huygens' wife could not rid herself of the shame she felt for her bare hands. She sent the maid on errands that were more suited to the woman of the house, and became autocratic in the face of the girl's growing pride. Her dress became more sombre and matronly, and she carried a bunch of keys at her belt.

Every night Huygens lifted the glass bell, tugged his wife's ring down as far as it would go, and left the clock ticking over the hearth.

Like Eve, Huygens' wife had been warned. The ring must not be pulled when the clock was striking the hour. At best, this would destroy the clock's chimes, at worst, she would break the endless chain and the weights would fall.

Her mistake came five years on, one night when Huygens was away. At least she said that he was away, even though he was at that moment taking off his boots in the hall. He was welcomed at the door by the clock striking midnight, a sound that always filled him with both love and pride. It struck five times and stopped.

There are many reasons why Huygens' wife pulled the ring at that moment. He put the action down to womanly foolishness. She was pregnant at the time and her mind was not entirely her own. It was because of her state and the tears that she shed that he left the ruined clock as it was and the remaining months of her lying-in were marked by the silence of the hours.

The boy was born and Huygens' wife lay with

childbed fever. In her delirium (it was still a time when women became delirious) she said only one thing, over and over again: 'I will die. He will die. I will die. He will die. I will die FIRST,' like a child picking the petals off a daisy. There were always five petals, and Huygens, whose head was full of tickings, likened her chant to the striking of a clock.

(But before you get carried away, I repeat, there were many reasons why Huygens' wife slipped her finger into the ring and pulled the chain.)

When his first wife died, Sir David Brewster was to be found at the desk in his study, looking out at the snow. In front of him was a piece of paper, very white, which was addressed to her father. On it was written 'Her brief life was one of light and grace. She shone a kindly radiance on all those who knew her, or sought her help. Our angel is dead. We are left in darkness once more.'

In Sir David's hand was a dull crystal which he held between his eye and the flaring light of the snow. As evening fell, the fire behind him and his own shape were reflected on the window, a fact which Sir David could not see, until he let the lens fall and put his head into his hands.

There was more than glass between the fire, Sir David and the snow outside.

There was a crystalline, easily cleavable and non-lustrous mineral called Iceland spar between the fire, Sir David and the snow, which made light simple. It was Sir David's life's work to bend and polarise light and he was very good at it. Hence the lack of reflection in his windows and the flat, non-effulgent white of the ground outside.

Of his wife, we know very little. She was called MacPherson and was the daughter of a famous (in his day) literary fraud. MacPherson senior was the 'translator' of the verse of Ossian, son of Fingal, a third-century Scottish bard – who existed only because the age had found it necessary to invent him. Ossian moped up and down the highlands, kilt ahoy, sporran and dirk swinging poetically, while MacPherson read passages of the Bible to his mother in front of the fire. MacPherson was later to gain a seat in the House of Commons.

All the same, his family must have found sentiment a strain, in the face of the lies he propagated in the world. I have no reason to doubt that his daughters sat at his knee or playfully tweaked his moustaches, read Shakespeare at breakfast with the dirty bits taken out, and did excellent needlepoint, which they sold on the sly. The problem is not MacPherson and his lies, nor Brewster and his optics. The problem is that they touched a life without a name, on the very fringes of human endeavour. The problem is sentimental. Ms MacPherson was married to the man who invented the kaleidoscope.

*

Kal eid oscope: Something beautiful I see. This is the simplest and the most magical toy; made from a tube and two mirrors, some glass and coloured beads.

The *British Cyclopaedia* describes the invention in 1833. 'If any object, however ugly or irregular in itself, be placed (in it) . . . every image of the object will coalesce into a form mathematically symmetrical and highly pleasing to the eye. If the object be put in motion, the combination of images will likewise be put in motion, and new forms, perfectly different, but equally symmetrical, will successively present themselves, sometimes vanishing in the centre, sometimes emerging from it, and sometimes playing around in double and opposite oscillations.'

The two mirrors in a kaleidoscope do not reflect each other to infinity. They are set at an angle, so that their reflections open out like a flower, meet at the bottom and overlap.

When she plays with it, her hand does not understand what her eye can see. It can not hold the secret size that the mirrors unfold.

She came down to London for the season and met a young man who told her the secrets of glass. The ballroom was glittering with the light of a chandelier that hung like a bunch of tears, dripping radiance over the dancers. She was, of course, beautiful, in this shattered light and her simple white dress.

He told her that glass was sand, melted in a white hot crucible: white sand, silver sand, pearl ash, powdered quartz. He mentioned glasswort, the plant from which potash is made; the red oxide of lead, the black oxide of manganese. He told her how arsenic is added to plate glass to restore its transparency, how a white poison made it clear.

Scientific conversation was of course fashionable at the time, and boredom polite, but David Brewster caught a spark in the young girl's eye that changed all these dull facts into the red-hot liquid of his heart.

He told her how glass must be cooled or it will explode at the slightest touch.

After their first meeting he sent her in a box set with velvet, Lacrymae Vitreae, or Prince Rupert's Drops: glass tears that have been dripped into water. In his note, he explained that the marvellous quality of these tears is that they withstand all kinds of force applied to the thick end, but burst into the finest dust if a fragment is broken from the thin end. He urged her to keep them safe.

Mr MacPherson's daughter and Dr (soon to be Sir) David Brewster were in love.

There is a difference between reflection and refraction, between bouncing light and bending it, between letting it loose and various, or twisting it and making it simple. As I mentioned before, Sir David's life's work was to make light simple, something he did for the glory of man and God. Despite the way her eyes sparkled when she smiled, and the molten state of his heart, Sir David's work was strenuous, simple and hard. He spent long hours computing angles, taking the rainbow apart.

Imagine the man of science and his young bride on their wedding night, as she sits in front of the mirror and combs her hair, with the light of candles playing in the shadows of her face. Perhaps there are two mirrors on the dressing table, and she is reflected twice. Perhaps it was not necessary for there to be two, in order for Sir David to sense, in or around that moment, the idea of the kaleidoscope; because in their marriage bed, new forms, perfectly different, but equally symmetrical, successively presented themselves, sometimes vanishing in the centre, sometimes emerging from it, and sometimes playing around in double and opposite oscillations.

(One of the most beautiful things about the kaleidoscope is, of course, that it is bigger on the inside. A simple trick which is done with mirrors.)

Perhaps because of the lives they led, these people had a peculiar fear of being buried alive. This resulted in a fashionable device which was rented out to the bereaved. A glass ball sat on the corpse's chest, and was connected, by a series of counterweights, pulleys and levers, to the air above. If the body started to breathe, the movement would set off the mechanism, and cause a white flag to be raised above the grave. White, being the colour of surrender, made it look as if death had laid siege, and failed.

Death laid early siege to the bed of Sir David Brewster and his wife. She was to die suitably; pale and wasted against the pillows, her translucent hand holding a handkerchief, spotted with blood. It was a time when people took a long time to die, especially the young.

It is difficult to say what broke her, a chance remark about the rainbow perhaps, when they were out for their daily walk, and he explained the importance of the angle of forty-two degrees. Or drinking a cup of warm milk with her father's book on her lap, and finding the skin in her mouth. Or looking in the mirror one day and licking it.

It was while she was dying that Sir David stumbled upon the kaleidoscope. He thought of her in the ballroom, when he first set eyes on her. He thought of her in front of the mirror. He built her a toy to make her smile in her last days.

When she plays with it, the iris of her eye twists and widens with delight.

Because of her horror of being buried alive, Sir David may have had his wife secretly cremated. From her bone-ash he caused to be blown a glass bowl with an opalescent white skin. In it he put the Lacrymae Vitreae, the glass tears that were his first gift. Because the simple fact was, that Sir David Brewster's wife was not happy. She had no reason to be.

Sir David was sitting in his study, with the fire dying in the grate, his lens of Iceland spar abandoned by his side. He was surprised to find that he had been crying, and he lifted his head slowly from his hands, to wipe away the tears. It was at that moment that he was visited by his wife's ghost, who was also weeping.

She stood between him, the window and the snow outside. She held her hands out to him and the image shifted as she tried to speak. He saw, in his panic, that she could not be seen in the glass, though he saw himself there. Nor was she visible in the mirror, much as the stories told. He noted vague shimmerings of colour at the edge of the shape that were truly 'spectral' in their nature, being arranged in bands. He also perceived, after she had gone, a vague smell of ginger in the room.

Sir David took this visitation as a promise and a sign. In the quiet of reflection, he regretted that he had not been able to view this spectral light through his polarising lens. This oversight did not, however, stop him claiming the test, in a paper which he wrote on the subject. Sir David was not a dishonest man, nor was he cold. He considered it one of the most important lies of his life. It was an age full of ghosts as well as science, and the now forgotten paper was eagerly passed from hand to hand.

*

Ruth's mother was deaf. Her mouth hung slightly ajar. When Ruth was small her mother would press her lips against her cheek and make a small, rude sound. She used all of her body when she spoke and her voice came from the wrong place. She taught Ruth sign language and how to read lips. As a child, Ruth dreamt about sound in shapes.

Sometimes her mother would listen to her through the table, with her face flat against the wood. She bought her a piano and listened to her play it through her hand. She could hear with any part of her body.

Of course she was a wonder child, clever and shy. Her own ears were tested and the doctor said 'That child could her the grass grow Mrs Rooney.' Her mother didn't care. For all she knew, the grass was loud as trumpets.

Her mother told Ruth not to worry. She said that in her dreams she could hear everything. But Ruth's own dreams were silent. Perhaps that was the real difference between them.

When Ruth grew up she started to make shapes that were all about sound. She wove the notes of the scale in coloured strings. She turned duration into thickness and tone into shade. She overlapped the violins and the oboe and turned the roll of the drum into a wave.

It seemed to Ruth that the more beautiful a piece of music was, the more beautiful the shape it made. She was a successful sculptor, who brought all of her work home to her mother and said 'Dream about this, Ma. Beethoven's Ninth.'

Of course it worked both ways. She could work

shapes back into the world of sound. She rotated objects on a computer grid and turned them into a score. This is the complicated sound of my mother sitting. This is the sound of her with her arm in the air. It played the Albert Hall. Her mother heard it all through the wood of her chair.

As far as people were concerned, friends and lovers and all the rest, she listened to them speak in different colours. She made them wonder whether their voices and their mouths were saying the same thing as their words, or something else. The whole message was suddenly complicated, involuntary and wise.

On the other hand, men never stayed with her for long. She caused the sound of their bodies to be played over the radio, which was, in its way, flattering. What they could not take was the fact that she never listened to a word they said. Words like: 'Did you break the clock?' 'Why did you put the mirror in the hot press?' 'Where is my shoe?'

'The rest is silence.'

When Ruth's mother was dying she said 'I will be able to hear in Heaven.' Unfortunately, Ruth knew that there was no Heaven. She closed her mother's eyes and her mouth and was overwhelmed by the fear that one day her world would be mute. She was not worried about going deaf. If she were deaf then she would be able to hear in her dreams. She was terrified that her shapes would lose their meaning, her grids their sense, her colours their public noise. When the body beside her was no longer singing, she thought, she might as well marry it, or die.

She really was a selfish bastard (as they say of men and angels).

Fruit Bait

The first tattoo was an audience in purple and green, with mouths that laughed when she lifted her arms. Never turn your back, the man told her as the last vermilion lost its sting. Spiders, fish, an octopus on her backside with a beak that opened and shut. She knew that the tattooist was mad when he talked to her about power, although she dreamt about applause all the time.

She woke up to an empty room and a bad smell from the sheets, dreamt again of a blind woman and her serving boy, faithful unto death.

A friend called at eleven o'clock and talked about people they knew. Pregnant women mostly, and men who couldn't make up their minds.

She slept again all afternoon and expected her body to be changed when she woke. The tattooist was there with a bouquet of flowers, tiger lilies on her hands and African violets in a chaplet on her thigh.

The street was full of opportunities for a natural-born hero: people to follow, messages on the path, a faint smell of kerosene in a back alley. The cars floated by like a movie and there could have been anyone at the wheel.

She bought a packet of cigarettes and then stole out of the shop, looking down the street for a man with a port wine stain, or a tear-shaped mole.

An old geezer accosted her over coffee and recognised her voice from an ad for the telephone. 'Reach out and touch . . .' he said, 'someone you love.'

'Have you paid your television licence?' she asked.

'Just relax with Johnson's tea,' he said. 'I can tell, you're an actress to your fingertips.'

'Well, to the tip of my tongue, anyway.'

That night her radio voice took on a face. She was a rich girl and the tattooist swabbed a blue veil over her belly with a *trompe l'œil* rococo façade on her thighs. A cherub on either breast flew when she lifted her arms. A friend knocked on her door at four in the morning and found her body clean as a sheet.

There was work on Wednesday. 'Style! Lift! Gel!' – another radio ad. She took the cheque and celebrated with a bag full of fruit which would catch the light on the table in her flat. Two hours were spent in a bookshop thinking about a volume of photographs that didn't have any people in it at all, then she walked the streets again, feeding herself and waiting for the applause. A woman walked by with tanned *décolletage* like a gift to the unwary and her perfect breasts seemed to laugh at her face.

The bag of fruit was beginning to weigh in her hand when she saw the man with the tear-shaped mole, that hung like a promise under one pea-green eye. He was dressed like an accountant and had large, uncomfortable hands. She trailed his sad back to the door of a firm in Merrion Square. (Oh boy. Right again.) As he walked up the steps she caught his arm. 'You must have dropped this . . .' putting a nectarine in his fist.

There was no sleep at all that night, but she made extensive plans to get her hair cut and start drinking again. She sat opposite the door in Merrion Square at lunchtime and dressed the passers-by in brocade and panniered petticoats. He came out at last, with the shadow of a fob watch swinging above his belt, and she rolled an orange at his feet as he walked along. He picked it up on his toe like a hurler and flipped it in to his hand then looked round before she was gone.

Apples, tangerines, peaches, a whole melon. By the end of the week she had bought a pineapple and the tattooist was going wild. There were birds all over her back singing in a tree with forked roots. He was causing her more pain. Blood was dabbed away with pieces of newspaper, and the earthquake on page seven cracked all over her torso when she tossed in her sleep. He turned her front into an armchair with a chintz design. And on the last night she foamed like the sea while a cormorant dived from her throat.

On Pineapple Day she dressed like Carmen Miranda, and walked around the square three times before settling by the door. The people passing by wore peacock hats and leopard-skin claws dangling at the throat when the man with the tear-shaped mole let himself out through the door. He kept his suit on, but the briefcase in his hand started to sprout as he walked past her down the steps. He turned in the street and faced her as she let the pineapple fall. It bounced from one step to the next and rolled to his feet.

Historical Letters

1.

So. I wouldn't wash the sheets after you left, like some tawdry El Paso love affair. No one is unhappy in El Paso. There is lithium in the water supply. So it all still smells of you and at four in the morning that's a stink and at five it's a desert hum, with cicadas blooming all over the ceiling. Because you are on the road.

I am not hysterical. We have mice – just to go with all this heat and poverty and lust business, two women with grown-up salaries and lives to run after. Actually, it is hot, which I hate. If I want weather I pay for it, besides, the sun only came out for you. Actually, also, there is something in the water supply.

I have prehensile toes because you made my feet grip like a baby's fist. That's not something you forget so easily.

*

You, on the other hand, do forget – easily and all the time. This is something I admire. You don't make up little stories to remember by. Which means that I am burdened with all the years that you passed through and neglected. I can handle them, of course, with my excellent synapses that feel no pain.

There is something about you that reminds me of the century. You talk like it was Before as well as After and you travel just to help you think – as if we were all still living in nineteen-hundred-and-sixty-five. There's nothing special about you, Sunshine, except how gentle you are. And you talk like it was nineteen-hundred-and-seventy-four. 'Live a quiet life, be true, try to be honest. Work, don't hurt people.' You said all this while putting on your socks, which were bottle-green, very slowly.

Sleeping with you is like watching a man in a wet suit cleaning windows, in with the otters on the other side.

All I want to say, before you disappear into that decade of yours, all I want to say is how things became relevant, how the sugar-bowl sits well on the table, how the wood seems to agree.

But it is a gift, like snow. It is a gift the way the bowl sits so well on the table, it is a gift how it all, including you, was pushed out through a cleft in time. Pop! I can move my hand from the bowl, over a fork, to my own blue cup, and the distance between them makes me content.

2.

You may say, in you turn, that I am an aquatic kind of girl, an underwater sort of thing. Since you left I spend most of my time on my back, as it were. I can see the street in a fan of light on the bedroom ceiling. When someone walks past, they move a line of shadow like the needle on a dial. Cars make everything shiver.

I remember most of what you said and I said. I don't see the point of this landscape of yours, blank and full of frights with no clock in it. All your pain strikes me as very nineteen-hundred-and-sixty-seven. I come from the generation that never took drugs, the generation that grew up. I am a woman that was born in 1962.

And you know what that means.

*

Despite the fact that I was born in nineteen-hundred-and-sixty-two, I go around the house mouthing words like they were new, like the whole problem of words was as fresh as Paris. You have infected me with the fifties, une femme d'un certain âge who knows how to dress but not how to speak. Sweetheart.

Tell me. When was the Spanish Civil War? Is that where you are? Having a serious discussion about reification and blood, rubbing alcohol and the future. I bet the people you meet all have stories, perplexities, Slavic bones.

When I was ten a white horse ran into the side of the school bus and died. I saw the blood bubble out of his nose.

You should go to Berlin in nineteen-hundred-and-eighty-nine, with the wall coming down. You could put the Cabaret and the Jews back in perhaps. I am there, watching it all on TV, getting everything wrong. I am wrong about remote-control televisions, denim, history in general. I can't tell where the party is. I do not have a democratic mind, but if I watch the right movie, the horse dies every time. (Why is it always white?)

*

So I am supposed to sit here with my finger in my gee until you come back – from Moscow in 1937 where you discover what music really is. From New Orleans in 1926 where you are eating the heart out of artichokes. From Dublin in 1914 where you are walking, pretentiously enough, on the beach. When I just got my credit cards, the sign of a woman who does not wait around.

History is just a scum on reality as far as you are concerned. You scrape it away.

Listen.

When de Valera died, I didn't care either way, but a girl in my class was delighted, because her granny was buried half an hour before him, and all the soldiers along the road saluted as they went by.

I saw them landing on the moon, but my mother wasn't bothered. She wanted to finish drying the dishes, so she said, 'Sure I can see the moon, right here in the window.'

When I was ten a white horse ran into the side of the school bus and died. I saw the blood bubble out of his nose.

That is what I want to say. I was not washed up on the beach of your life like Venus on the tide. I know the distance between the cup and the bowl. I have seen

Berlin. I have seen the moon. I will find out how to speak again and change the sheets, because it must change, I say, in order to give pleasure.

Never mind the horse.

Eckhardt's Dream

Eckhardt dreamt of installing television sets in his room that had nothing to do with the common man. He would play them himself like organ stops. He would pass them by in a yellow light and the light in the television sets would be blue. The decor in his room left much to be desired.

In front of one curtain he would put a set that showed a picture of the curtain. Beside it, its neighbour and twin would show a picture of the curtain on fire.

This is where Eckhardt began to lose the dream. He moved to the opposite window, which had the same curtain, with the same brown and yellow stripe. This he would pull to the ground. In front of it, a television set would show: the dead rumpled mass of the curtain on the floor, and a view of the night outside. Beside it, its neighbour and twin was broken. Eckhardt had smashed the tube. It showed nothing at all, but behind it, the window showed something plötzlich, unbekannt.

*

And the moral of the dream is: Eckhardt lived with his girlfriend and his dog and sometimes he loved the dog more.

Fatgirl Terrestrial

Why could she never find herself a public man? A man to walk down the street with, a man who would tend to the barbecue and flirt lightly with her friends. The fact that she was fat might have something to do with it (though she had no trouble scoring); the fact that she was fat and so felt herself to be odd; the fact that she was fat and so felt herself to be beyond the pale – free. Because every man she found was perfect at the time, perfect within her four walls or his, but, without exception, they all fell apart when she put them on display. Perhaps she was not sufficiently odd. Maybe there was an insubordinate streak of the ordinary in her, a thin woman trying to get out.

Successful women are supposed to be fat, she decided early on. If they are trim and look like mistresses then the board room is a minefield. She developed a motherly laugh. She developed a viciousness that made people mutter 'Fat bitch' and 'No wonder she's so neurotic – would you look at the size of her,' as their assignments came in on time.

She liked sleeping with men. It changed them. They were always surprised by her body – fat being a novelty they would never have thought to pursue. They became nostalgic in her bed for first loves that had been reared on bread and dripping, for soft, Victorian thighs and garter belts that made a dent. They protested that sexuality was all to do with flesh – they were tired of being told to lust after skin and bone. Even so, their young wives were thin and expensive-looking. Bridget had noticed over the years that fat girls were expected to be cheaper and often went halves on dates. She didn't mind. She had plenty of money.

The men from work were not public men. They had nine-to-five faces and girlfriends who worked out. She could feel herself inflating when they walked into the room.

Nevertheless she confused them by her indifference and by the lack of conspiracy in her smile. Good-looking ones were the worst. They wanted Bridget to fall in love and bother them in the canteen with Significant and Resentful Looks. They avoided her ostentatiously and became helpful, formal and efficient.

One of the great sadnesses of Bridget's life was the fact that it all looked so sleek. Underneath the hard and friendly manner of a fatgirl who made it against the odds was the commonplace sickness of a woman who wanted a serious man. It was in public that the nausea hit – because there was a whole rake of oddities that Bridget did risk herself with. Men with sweaty eyes who liked to hold her hand walking down a street and were dying to meet her friends.

Her friends had a taste in wired, artistic-looking

types who liked to talk about themselves; men who could make an impression. Joan was addicted to the married variety and could not shake it, Maggie was interested in sex for its own sake, and Sunniva was pure class. Bridget adored and respected all three. She loved a good laugh and the privacy of their nights out. She was nearly jealous of their men, even though she knew that they were private disasters. These socially easy and uniformly handsome beasts used Maggie, Sunniva and Joan like bust-up sofas or wore them down with snideness and superficiality. There were tearful confessions of violence or infidelity. But when they all went out for the night no one had a bad time. Even their shirts were witty and they insisted on buying all the drinks.

Bridget divided her disasters into sections and phases. There were the fanatics, who had a tight, neurotic smell and undiluted eyes. They talked about death all the time or were severely political. There were the outright freaks: bizarre, hairy or double-jointed men who played the saw on the streets or trained to be anaesthetists; men who hated themselves so badly they might injure themselves if left on their own in a room. Some respite was provided by the silent brigade: patriarchal countrymen or foreigners, with rings of perspiration under the arms of their shirts and mothers who ascended bodily into heaven. There were the endearingly stupid. Men with beautiful smiles, who felt up Joan, or Maggie or even Sunniva under various tables and made obscene suggestions with cheerful tenacity and loping Woody Allen eyes.

Bridget made all the more usual and banal mistakes though they never lasted long: alcoholics, virgins, latent homosexuals, 'artists', whores, seminarian types, and one man who never spoke at all, who was mortified by the sound of female laughter.

The disaster was that Bridget loved them all. She loved them for wanting to hold her hand walking down a street, even though she was fat. She loved them because she knew that she was odd, despite the motherly laugh, the linen suits and the way she said 'Oh my aching feet!' to the person she sat down next to on the bus.

The life of an optimist is a lonely one. Bridget collected seashells and bits of blue glass in walks along the beach. Once a week she visited her elderly mother who had a medical pragmatism about sex. If Bridget did not find a husband soon then her insides would wither away and have to be removed. Of course when your daughter is thirty-five and a professional woman one doesn't enquire too deeply into her affairs, but in her mother's eyes Bridget was too fat for casual sex. She was, however, with her apartment, her job, and her motherly laugh, a Fine Catch. So there was a chance that some lonely and sensible man would save her womb from ossification in the grateful boredom of the marriage bed.

Bridget's mother believed in the marriage bed. When she was not talking about unmentionable diseases she was busy flirting with her dead husband. Bridget's dreams after these visits became infested with her father's eyes. She remembered the day that the world fell apart and her mother's secret store of cosmetics was found. He made one of his only visits into the shops in town with the bag in his hand, went into the make-up counter in Switzers and demanded an estimate of prices from the assistant in her startling white coat. He fined the total from her mother's housekeeping money, with interest. At his funeral, Bridget's mother was plastered so thick with make-up that the mourners took her for some secret mistress, grinned with pride for the dead man and looked the other way.

Bridget was doing her best. She made a conscientious search for the lonely and sensible man. She sat in café windows and watched young and old pass by. She looked at their backs and asked 'Is that a sensible bottom? Can you tell by their taste in socks?' But she knew as she examined them in supermarkets or in traffic jams that she was a hopeless case. Any number of men with nine-to-five minds could provoke her into a faint stir of heat – but it was the ones that twitched who turned her inside out. These she would follow and catch with an audacity that made them feel needed. She would bring them back and empty them out all over her flat. She made them tea, folded them into her, wiped away their hurts and talked them dry – until they were so wet-eyed in love with her that her breasts began to swell. She held their taste in her mouth through the day and laughed all over the office. She started to speak their language.

All would be well until they grew suspicious of this interior life. They had to find out why she wanted them and who she was. They stood outside her office at six o' clock and asked to meet her friends. They claimed her, laughed abnormally and let their jealously show.

Even her friends were settling down, and their evenings out took on an alien air. Joan's latest married man was on the brink of leaving his wife and moving in, with his green eyes and excellent tailor. Maggie decided that sex was nothing without procreation and had a child by some Casanova who reformed on the spot and started to dote. Sunniva decided at last on a quiet civil servant who was a dedicated cook, read three books a week and adored her. Bridget, meanwhile, met a small travel agent with dog-brown eyes whom she thought might do.

She was initially attracted by a sign in his window which read 'Have a Boring Holiday Instead. Do Absolutely Nothing in Kinsale. Gourmet Food.'

She appeared to him in her most attractive persona, very slow and very witty and he appeared to her as light and hungry. The matter was soon resolved.

For some reason she did not despise the travel agent. There was something secret about his body, as though it were invisibly tattooed and wild beneath his suit. It made his business clothes seem like some kind of perversion – as though the tweed were a step more dangerous than latex, and she undressed him with care. He was perfectly presentable, willing, witty, he had a good singing voice, and the charming face of a sexual child. Just when Bridget thought she had found it at last – the exciting, ordinary man – the travel agent showed her his collection of dolls.

The travel agent was a witch. He insisted that the word was 'warlock' but she couldn't see him in a sky-blue cloak scattered with stars. He believed in everything that was going, and a little bit more: astrology, herbs, zombie voodoo, Nietzsche, shamans, omens, some Buddhism and the fact that Bridget had been a water-buffalo and a Creole Madame in previous lives.

He talked to her about animal spirits and shape-changing with a ferocity that clashed with his lemon-yellow tie, and they followed discussions about telepathy and childhood with arguments about whether the bill should go on his expenses or hers. She gave him a key to her flat and he would turn up in the middle of the night with the strangest smells on his skin.

Bridget lived in an apartment block with a failing popular singer upstairs, two widows on either side, and someone who worked in TV below. She changed lightbulbs for the widows and they watered her potted plants. She met the failing popular singer in the hall with glitter on her cheeks, and listened to her sobbing through the ceiling all night. The TV person was rarely there and she did her crying in the mornings. Bridget and the widows never cried. As her affaire with the travel agent progressed, a flicker came into the widows' eyes and they started to borrow more cups of sugar. Slowly the apartment filled up with feathers, beads, small sweaty pieces of paper with mysterious and banal phrases leaking in the creases and the occasional mask. Bridget believed. Why shouldn't she? She believed because the travel agent said that it didn't matter whether she believed or not. All these facts were indifferent to her, as the animals are, and they spoke a different language. As the travel agent said, when you are talking about Power the word 'true' had about the same weight as the word 'orange'. She started worrying about flights of crows, and wrote small hexes to put under his pillow.

The travel agent spent late nights grinding out his philosophies, trying to make her afraid of the dark. He started at hawk shadows on the walls and said that her body was a landscape of mist with a creature in it he could not meet. He begged her to howl and grunt, and the widows' hands started to tremble with admiration as she filled their cups with borrowed flour.

In point of fact, Bridget did feel herself to be under a spell. He flipped her body on the bed like a cake in a pan, he sang messages onto her answering machine. At inappropriate moments she would see him smile at the door, and when she looked, he wasn't there.

There must have been one particular morning when Bridget first neglected to take her shower. It was probably a morning in spring, which was always her most anxious time. Spring made her think of summer and her inability to wear shorts. The crocuses and the daffodils started pushing their way into her mind, like the sound of a party to which she had not been invited.

The thin light made her pant going up the stairs and left a turbid scum on all her windows. It was the time when she forgot to like her fat. It was the time when she most distrusted the fact that she was odd.

She asked the travel agent to marry her and he rolled over onto his back in the bed, stared into the dark and said yes. This was shortly before he noticed that dust was gathering in the shower head and her potted plants were all starting to die. As for the smell, he didn't seem to mind.

There were other creaks and groans on her way to a final halt. Bridget was bright as a button at work in the same dress all week, although she changed hats from day to day. The hats were needed to hide the beehive of tangles she got from writhing on her back underneath the travel agent, which she somehow wasn't interested in combing away. There were wrinkled noses and whispered complaints, but her bosses were all men, so none of them took her aside for a few words. Besides, Bridget had started to lose weight.

Maggie, Joan and Sunniva knew a crisis when they saw one, although it was three weeks before they invaded, cut Bridget's hair short, made her a meal and ran the bath. They all got splendidly pissed and made plans for the wedding, which for Bridget's sake, and the state she was in, would have to be fast or not at all. Joan said not at all, but Bridget said Yes at all costs. Sunniva agreed and made a pact with Bridget to 'pull herself together'. Maggie demanded that she get pregnant to make the union meaningful and all of them asked 'My God Bridget, what IS he like?' 'He's a bit odd,' she answered. 'He's magic,' and they laughed until four o'clock in the morning.

Bridget realised the need for secrecy. Both her lapses and her man must be kept secret from the rest of the world. Her smell without water settled down and she chose a musky perfume to compliment it and make it more modern. She made the effort to dress and moved without complaint to the backwaters of the firm. Her short hair explained the new smallness of her face.

The travel agent seemed to be avoiding her except in the hours of darkness. He said that he loved her. He slit his finger and left a small bowl of blood beside her bed. There was a feather in the bowl.

One day she caught sight of him on the street and the ease with which he walked and talked was a minor miracle. He was wearing a shirt with thick blue-and-white stripes and an all-white collar. He had a blue paisley tie. His blue-grey jacket was slung over his shoulder by the maker's tag. (Unfortunately he was wearing brown shoes, but she took that as an exterior sign.) There were two men walking beside him in similar suits, one in navy blue, one in grey. They were bigger than him, but their bodies were sloppy. All their attention was devoted to what he was saying and they laughed a lot. She was hopelessly in love with that man.

Maggie, Sunniva and Joan took care of arrangements while she took to her bed with the shadow of a hawk now real on the wall and wolf howls in the middle of the night. When things were very bad she went back to her fat laugh and her slow, witty talk. She pretended to listen a lot. Her days were spent in prescribed sets of movements, and when she erred – if, for example, she put her shoes on before her blouse – then she was made to suffer badly. She got cramps and side-stitches, shadows flitted and tormented her. Sometimes when she sat still there was music in the room that made her want to cry.

At night she dreamt of all the men she had loved, who queued by her bedside, and laid red, dark bunches of grapes in her lap.

Bridget got married in an ivory satin dress with a bouquet of freesias and the wedding march thundering down the aisle. Maggie, Joan and Sunniva cried their eyes out while her mother concentrated on the invisible knitting in her lap. Joe (for that was the travel agent's name) unveiled fifty-three relatives of impeccable respectability. Several nuns were in evidence, their hair unveiled and neatly styled. The women wore huge and expensive dresses in various sheens of acrylic, with splattered prints and enormous shoulder pads. They rustled and sagged in the church benches, sighing for their youth and the Day They Had Done It. The men were all backslappers, continually checked in their talk by the echoes from the vaulted roof, and they turned around in their seats, mouthing vigorous reminders of stag nights and holes of golf to each other, with jovial incomprehensibility.

Bridget trembled violently as she entered the church, after being held for ten minutes for photographs in the freezing cold of the porch. Her arms were purple and poked out of her dress like chicken legs. She clutched at the uncle delegated to give her away, as his chin went double with the formal effort of the long walk. Her progress was met with the traditional indulgence and good humour, and there was a great sigh from the bride's side when they saw how thin, how marvellous she looked. Joe waited for her in front of a Victorian Gothic altar, dapper in his morning suit, hands folded neatly, fingernails manicured and buffed to a slight shine.

She had a violent sexual tic when she felt the wool of his sleeve. What was under his suit? A bleeding sign slashed into his belly? A word on his breast? Or nothing at all? He smiled and so did she.

The priest was a malaria victim back from the missions who got her name wrong twice, though not at the vital moments. His sermon drifted back to the savannah as he lifted his eyes to the ceiling and talked to the simple black souls he saw there. He advised Joe against taking two wives.

When it came to the exchange of rings, Bridget was solid again. She could feel the ground under her feet and she didn't get his name wrong. Her hands, she noticed, as he placed the ring, were thin and expensive-looking.

*

At the reception Joe was the life and soul. Maggie, Sunniva and Joan could hardly contain their enthusiasm as they flirted with him beyond the call of duty. They were shy of expressing their surprise to Bridget, who was shrouded with the new privacy of a married woman, even to her friends. Of course she had married a normal man. How could they have expected a disaster?

Maggie got maudlin and cried as she said over and over 'I always knew you were beautiful. I always knew.'

Bridget wasn't used to looking so well. She danced with all of Joe's uncles and three of them made a fumble as they let her go. She got too much attention.

Her sixteen-year-old cousin tried to seduce Sunniva's civil servant and there was a tight little scene in the ladies' toilet. In the corner, the mother of the bride had three brandies, gave a polite rendition of 'Goodnight Irene' and told anyone who would listen about the horrors of a life spent with a mean man.

Through it all, Joe kept his eye on her, smiled and lusted sedately. They met amongst the dancers and he said 'How are you? Alright?' and squeezed her hand like a brave girl.

'Wait until he gets you home Oho ye Boya!' said one of the uncles and Joe's teeth glittered as he smiled.

The D.J. hustled them into a ring to sing 'Congratulations'. He said 'Only virgins leave at nine o'clock, but a little birdie told me that they wanted to go.' Joe singed him with a look.

The bouquet was thrown and it landed in the chandelier, which would not stop swinging.

Joan whispered 'Don't forget the garter.' and Bridget felt a burning sensation on her thigh.

They were forced to run the gauntlet and Bridget was bruised by her mother as she attempted and missed a first and last kiss. Outside, the street was on fire with reflected neon that lit her dress in red, then blue. 'Jesus Christ, this is it,' said Bridget as she ripped off her veil and pinned it to the car aerial. The toilet paper flapped and everybody cheered as Bridget was driven into the thin, wet night by her public man.

What are Cicadas?

Cold women who drive cars like the clutch was a whisper and the gear stick a game. They roll into petrol stations, dangle their keys out the window and say 'Fill her up' to the attendant, who smells of American Dreams. They live in haciendas with the reek of battery chickens out the back, and their husbands are old. They go to Crete on their holidays, get drunk and nosedive into the waiter's white shirt saying 'I love you Stavros!' even though his name is Paul. They drive off into a countryside with more hedges than fields and are frightened by the vigour of their dreams.

But let us stay, as the car slides past, with the pump attendant; with the weeping snout of his gun, that drips a silent humiliation on the cement; with the smell of clean sharp skies, of petrol and of dung. The garage behind him is connected in tight, spinning triangles as his eyes check one corner and then the next. There is an old exhaust lying on a shelf in the wall, there is a baseball hat stiff with cobwebs, hanging in the black space over the door. There is a grave dug in the floor, where the boss stands with a storm lamp, picking at the underside of cars. Evenly spaced in the thick, white light that circles from the window are rings set in the stone, to tether cows long dead.

He has a transistor radio. He has a pen from Spain with a Señorita in the casing who slides past a toreador and a bull, until she comes to rest under the click, waiting for his thumb. He has a hat, which he only wears in his room.

He is a sensitive young man.

What are cicadas? Are they the noise that happens in the dark, with a fan turning and murder in the shadows on the wall? Or do they bloom? Do people walk through forests and pledge themselves, while the 'cicadas' trumpet their purple and reds all around?

It is a question that he asks his father, whose voice smells of dying, the way that his mother's smells of worry and of bread.

They look up the dictionary. ' "Cicatrise," ' says his father, who always answers the wrong question – ' "to heal; to mark with scars" – I always thought that there was only one word which encompassed opposites, namely. . . ? To cleave; to cleave apart as with a sword, or to cleave one on to the other, as in a loyal friend. If you were older we might discuss "cleavage" and whether the glass was half empty or half full. Or maybe we can have our cake and eat it after all.'

When he was a child, he asked what a signature tune was. 'A signature tune,' said his father, 'is a young swan-song – just like you. Would you look at him.'

He searched in the mirror for a clue. But his eyes just looked like his own eyes, there was no word for them, like 'happy' or 'sad'.

'Why don't cabbages have nerves?'

'A good question.' His father believed in the good question, though the answer was a free-for-all.

If he was asked where his grief began, or what he was grieving for, he would look surprised. Grief was this house, the leaking petrol pump, the way his mother smiled. He moved through grief. It was not his own.

He read poetry in secret and thought his mind was about to break. Sunset fell like a rope to his neck. The Señorita slid at her own pace past the man and the bull and nothing he could do would make her change.

*

'Come and do the hedges on Wednesday afternoon,' said a woman, as he handed her keys back through the window. Then she swept off through the hedges with the exhaust like an insult. The car had been full of expensive smells, plastic and perfume, hairspray, the sun on the dashboard. The lines around her eyes were shiny and soft with cream. Her skin reminded him of the rice-paper around expensive sweets, when you wet it in your mouth.

He rehearsed in his room until he was ready, then came and did the work. He hated her for her laugh at the door. 'It's only money,' she said, 'it won't bite.'

In years to come he would claim an ideal childhood, full of fresh air and dignity, the smell of cooking, rosehips and devil's bread in the ditch. On a Saturday night his sisters would fight by the mirror by the door and talk him into a rage, for the fun.

'The place was full of secrets. You wouldn't believe the secrets, the lack of shame that people had. Children that were slow, or uncles that never took their hands out of their trousers, sitting in their own dirt, money under the bed, forgetting how to talk anymore. It wasn't that they didn't care, filth was only filth after all. It was the way they took it as their own. There was no modesty behind a closed door, no difference, no meaning.'

To tell the truth, he did not go back for the money, although he knew the difference between a pound note and nothing at all. His pride drove him back, and the words of the man under the hat in his room. 'Give her what she wants.'

There was a small girl playing football on the grass, just to annoy. They knew each other from school. 'Your father is a disgrace,' she said in a grown-up voice. 'A disgrace, in that old jacket.' Then she checked the house for her mother and ran away. The woman sat knitting in the sun and watched him through the afternoon. Her back was straight and hands fast. She kept the window open, as if the smell of chicken slurry was fresh air.

She touched him most by her silence. The kitchen was clean and foreign, the hill behind it waiting to be cleared of thorns and muck. It was the kind of house that was never finished, that the fields did not want. It sat on a concrete ledge, like a Christmas cake floating out to sea.

He liked the precision of things, the logic of their

place, the way the cups made an effort as they sat on the shelf. There were some strays, here and there, an Infant of Prague forgotten on the back of the cooker, a deflated football wedged behind the fridge. The cistern from an old toilet was balanced against the back wall, although the bowl was gone.

Waiting for his cup of tea, he forgot what it was he had come for. She was ordinary at the sink, ordinary and sad as she took out the sugar and the milk. When she sat down in her chair at the far side of the room, she was old and looked impatient of the noise his spoon made against the cup.

She asked after his mother, and turned on the radio and said he made a good job of cutting the lawn with the grass still damp. They listened to the tail-end of the news and she took a tin down from the cupboard. 'I suppose I can trust you,' she said grimly as she opened it up and a swirl of pound notes was seen, like something naked and soft. There was music on the radio.

He fought for the pictures in his room, of a man with a hat, who casually takes her by the wrist and opens out the flat of her palm, as if he understood it. He thought of the taste of rice-paper melting on his tongue, of the things she might wear under her dress. He struggled for the order of things that might happen if he held his breath. She gave him an indifferent smile. He did not understand.

'Women,' said his father, 'torture us with contradiction, but just because they enjoy it, doesn't mean that it's not true.'

There was a soft scratching at the door, and the two of them froze as though caught, with the money trapped in the woman's hand. When it opened he saw an old, fat crone who would not cross the threshold. Her shape was all one, he couldn't tell where one bit ended and the next began. There was a used tissue caught in the palm of her hand. She had a shy face. 'Monica, is the creamery cart come?' 'Yes,' said the woman in a loud voice. 'It's a tanker, not a cart.' 'Oh no,' said the old woman 'I'm fine, don't worry about me.' She closed the door on herself without turning away.

Her name was Monica. She smiled at him, in complicity and shame. 'Deaf as a post,' she said, and the room dilated with the possibilities in her voice. She was embarrassed by the money in her hand. She looked at the bob of panic in his throat.

'There was a woman lived up the way from us, the kind

that had all the young fellas in a knot. You could tell she wanted something, though probably not from you. She was ambitious, that was the word. It wasn't just sex that gave her that look – like she knew more than you ever could. That she might tell you, if she thought you were up to it. She had an old husband in the house with her, and a mother, senile, deaf, who pottered around and got in the way. And one day the old woman died.

'My father came in from the removal, rubbing his hands. He was a mild kind of man. "Sic transit," he said. "Sic, sic, sic." He took off the old coat with a kind of ceremony. I remember him taking the rosary beads out of his pocket and putting them beside the liquidiser, which was their place. I remember how ashamed I was of him, the patches on his coat and the beads and the useless Latin. When he sat down he said "How the mighty," and I felt like hitting him.

'When someone died, this woman Maureen would wash the body, which was no big deal. She might take any basin they had in the house and a cloth – maybe the one they used for the dishes. I don't know if she got paid, maybe it was just her place.

' "The secrets of the dead," said Da, "and the house smelling of fresh paint. Oh but that's not all." He told me one of those country stories that I never want to hear; stories that take their time, and have a taste to them. Stories that wait for the tea to draw and are held over when he can't find the biscuits. "Do you know her?" he said, and I said I did. "A fine woman all the same, with a lovely pair of eyes in her head. As I remember." He remembered the mother too of course and what kind of eyes she had in her head, as opposed to anywhere else.

'It was the son-in-law broke the news that the old woman had died, and when Maureen came to lay out the corpse, she found the man in the kitchen reading a newspaper and the wife saying nothing, not even crying. She offered her condolences, and got no sign or reply. There was no priest in the house. So Maureen just quietly ducked her head down, filled a basin at the sink, tiptoed her way across the lino with the water threatening to spill. When she got to the door of the old woman's room the wife suddenly lifted her head and said "You'll have a cup of tea, Maureen, before you start."

'The corpse was on the bed, newly dead, but rotting all the same. The sheets hadn't been changed for a year so you couldn't tell what colour they should have been. She had . . . lost control of her functions but they just left her to it, so her skin was the same shade as the sheets. Maureen cut layers and layers of skirts and tights and muck off her and when she got to the feet, she nearly cried. Her nails had grown so long without cutting, they had curled in under the soles and left scars.

' "Those Gorman women," said my father, with relish. "So which of them came first, the chicken or her egg?" and he laughed at me like a dirty old codger on the side of the road.'

After he left the house, the sun was so strong, it seemed to kill all sound. He met her daughter on the road and tackled her for the football, then kicked it slowly into the ditch.

'When I lost my virginity, everything was the same, and everything was changed. I stopped reading poetry, for one thing. It wasn't that it was telling lies – it just seemed to be talking to someone else.

'Now I can't stop screwing around. What can I say? I hate it, but it still doesn't seem to matter. I keep my life in order. My dry-cleaning bill is huge. I have money.

'My father knew one woman all his life. He dressed like a tramp. Seriously. What could he know? He knew about dignity and the weather and words. It was all so easy. I hate him for landing me in it like this – with no proper question and six answers to something else.'

The Brat

She was a brat. It wasn't that she was good-looking – she could be, but she wasn't. She wore her ugliness like a badge. Her clothes were tight in all the worst places, but she pushed her body forward as she spoke. She had fat arms and small breasts. She wore bovver boots and cheap pink cotton trousers. She was all wrong. Her eyebrows were plucked bare and a thin, brown line was pencilled in over the stubble. There was a flicker in her eye that told you she knew that she was being watched, and every gesture took on the slight edge of performance. It made her unpopular, except with new acquaintances, whom she seduced casually and then annoyed.

Clare was fifteen. She had been drunk once in her life, with a girl from school who had filled two pint glasses with the top of every bottle on her parents' cupboard. They drank it all in one go and Clare noticed nothing until she sat down in the bus and discovered that her legs were numb. The rest of the night was spent throwing up in the queue for a toilet, and kissing a boy who took her home. When she woke up her eyes were swollen, and her father had left without his breakfast.

Clare's father makes his way from the Customs House to O'Beirne's on the Quays, crosses the Liffey by means of a bridge, so sited as to add to the distance between the two buildings a length of nearly three hundred yards.

'If I could swim now, I'd be right.' He is a man much given to speaking aloud when company is absent, and to silence when the nicer of social obligations might urge him into speech. Those contributions he does make are as counterpoint to the sounds of liquid consumption only, the sweetest of which is the sound of a pint drawing creamily at the bar, a music only those born with the gift, or those who spend a minimum of three thousand hours acquiring the gift, can hear.

O'Donnel was doubly blessed. He was born with a magic thumb, the sucking of which enabled him to discern the music of a good pint from the discord of a bad, before a head had even begun to form; but being a man of diligence and application (those same qualities which, combined with tenacity, ensured his promotion to the rank of Under-Manager, Grade Two of Dublin Corporation, Sanitation Section, despite the vagaries of political influence, which was never behind him, the unenlightened reservations of his superiors, cognisant as they were of his talents, and thence careful of their own interests and tenure, and the constant, whingeing begrudgery of his fellow workers, craven in the envy of a magnitude only the true culchie could muster, with the smell of dung still clinging to their boots, the stripes of the diocesan fathers still stinging their palms and the sly post-colonialism still giving the edge of flattery to every utterance of a personal nature that crossed their lips), he distrusted the gifts of nature and concentrated the subtle power of his intelligence on discerning, without the aid of his cool, Fenian thumb, that crystalline hum, that black, creamy noise, of a pint just waiting to be drunk.

The river is at an ebb, its green is black in the early evening. 'It's not green. See?' he says to a passing young woman, who ignores both him and the complexity of his literary allusion. He pivots his body and fixes his eyes on her receding back, its cheap, smart blue coat, her black hair and the hurried motion of her tights, with a pattern of skin disease, arranged in bows along the seam.

'Golden stockings she had on,' he says loudly, in the interests of the general good. A sharp sniff, and the air stings his nose, outside and in. Three fingers he counts, tapping them one after the other on the interstice of his right nostril.

'Most high, most pure, most sweet . . .' Black hair, blue coat, and flesh-coloured legs – don't forget the bows. He stands, swaying slightly against the flood of people crossing the river to the northside of the city and strains to hear the broken clack of her shoes on the pavement. He sees her opening cans in a bedsit in Drumcondra. The shoes are loose, and a raw, reddened heel emerges at every step.

'There will be peace in the valley,' he assures her and all the other backs now interrupting his view of her, as a benediction, then turns to square himself against the tide.

'I wouldn't spit now,' he says, 'at a pint. If it was handed to me.' He was a man who could not abide spit.

O'Donnel avoids the snug in O'Beirne's, likely as it is to contain Elements. He takes his place with the dockers at the bar.

'Stevedores.'

There is no need for another word, his order is known. The brown suit strains tightly against the yoke of his back as he places the elbows, long stained with old porter, carefully on two beer-mats equidistant from the apex of his nose. His head is loosely cupped in two large hands.

'There's one for the drip,' says the barman, slapping a mat under the point of his snout. O'Donnel stares at the wood of the counter, his feet broadly placed on the brass rail. His air could be interpreted as one of dignified rebuke.

'Larry,' he says, from the cavern of his crouched torso, 'would you ever hinge that elbow in the way God intended.' And not wishing to disturb the barman by his tone, he adds the phrase, 'he says,' to allow a proper distance from the remark.

'Does he so?' says Larry, and places a small preliminary Bushmills on the central mat.

After many hours of similar silences, the air is punctuated by the single word 'Nevermore'.

The barman gives the wink to a man in the snug, the

long-suffering recipient of countless memos on the subject of parking meters: the cleaning thereof, embellished in O'Donnel's hand by the appropriate quotations from the Latin.

'So they finally gave the old codger the push, eh?' The final syllable is terse, sympathetic, way-of-the-worldish; harsh, without interrogative cadence or function.

'Resigned, Larry. For God's sake, the word is "resigned".' He salutes the barman with his pint, and with one finger he taps, three times, on the interstice of his left nostril.

Clare was late home again. A boy came up to her at the dance and started asking questions. 'How are you?' 'What did the Da say?' It was the one she had kissed some weeks before and she found herself answering quite sweetly because of the shame she felt. She must have told him everything. 'You were crying,' he told her, 'and you said that you wanted to die.'

'I wanted to throw up,' she said.

'You did.'

'Well that didn't stop you, anyway.'

'Shush,' he said, although the music was making them shout, and she started to kiss him again.

He had a good, strong accent and spoke very carefully. When the slow songs came on he just stood back and looked at her face. They only kissed again when the music changed.

Apart from that he had green eyes. 'Don't fucking worry about me,' Clare said, 'I'm clever.'

'I know you're clever.'

'My father is clever.'

'My Da's an arsehole,' he said, 'So what?' He was like a doctor, he asked questions that no one else asked. Whatever it was that made him sad made him kind as well and so she took his sympathy. He was a nice man. She felt obliged to tell him things, like she would tell any unicorn she met in the street.

Clare's father was sitting in front of the television when she got home, with his eyes closed. He looked away from her when she came in, and examined the curtains. 'Words,' he said, 'are for the radio. They should have stuck to silent films. Where were you?'

'Where were you?' she asked back.

'Your mother never left, you know . . .' his voice trailed after her as she left the room, 'you have her accusatory tone to perfection.'

There was a smell in the house. Clare had never realised that the disinfectants, the carpet cleaners, the plastic boxes that were hung up in the toilet did any good. She had hated their stink, like an industrial version of all the fluids, lotions, perfumes and bath-salts that made it her mother's house. A stink of unnecessary work and hours spent in front of the mirror, of cleaning windows in pink fluffy slippers, of fits of hysteria when towels were folded the wrong way. Now the kitchen smelt of old fat, the hall of damp and urine, her bedroom of clothes come out of the rain, like the top deck of the bus on a bad morning.

She went across to pull the curtains and was shocked to see that the boy was still outside, his arms folded and leaning on top of the wall. He saw her, smiled and walked away.

Her brother came into the room, and she let the curtain drop. 'The old man got the sack,' he said. 'Where were you?'

Your honour, on this, the second occasion, the victim spent some hours with the accused outside her house. Interglottal activity was engaged upon and some saliva was exchanged. The couple embraced warmly and muscular tissue from the sacral region to the crown of the head was palpated. This was followed by both visual and tactile exploration of the upper limbs and face of the accused and there was a Verbal Exchange. On the evening in question the victim had his back to a wall and indentations made from the ornamental gravel in his buttocks and upper back took thirty minutes to diffuse.

A girl from up the road street told Clare that she had seen her mother in town, walking down the street 'and Dressed To Kill'.

Kill what?

It was on the third occasion that the alleged murder took place. I will not offend the court with details save that there were several breaks for cigarettes, which were smoked in a car, the windows of which, much to the amusement of the accused, became steamed up, in the manner of comic sketches which can be seen from time to time on the television set. I have the assurance of the victim that no reproductive processes were engaged, although they were vigorously and callously primed by the frotteur.

(Objection your honour! The term 'frottage' implies guilt, I will not have my client tried by lexiphanicism, at the hands of a coprolalomaniac!)

(Objection sustained.) The appalling psychological damage suffered by the victim even before the fatal blow was struck, can only be imagined, and in happier times this frustration of biology might be viewed in the light which it deserves and sentence passed commensurate with the enormity of the crime.

He had left school young. He had a car and a job. He had taken his hand off the wheel and crossed his middle finger over his index and said 'I'm like that. You see? You can trust me. I'm like that.' The streetlamp outside the house made slits of his eyes, and Clare was shocked by the freedoms she took. She was violent and tender and made herself cry again. He absorbed it all without surprise.

At three o'clock in the morning, she heard the sound of a dog barking and her father's voice. He was walking down the street with a Jack Russell at his heel. As she watched she saw that he was not kicking the dog but playing with it. He emerged from Mrs Costello's forsythia bush with only a few leaves in his hands, but he threw them defiantly, shouting 'Fetch!' The dog was confused and he bent down over it, flinging his arm out and repeating the command. Then he straightened up and addressed the street and its dog, in the grand manner: 'Bitch!' He buttoned up his coat and walked on.

'That's the old man,' she said to the boy in the car, who smiled.

'Does he have a shotgun?'

Clare had never seen her father look monumental. He staggered in and out of the light from the streetlamp and she lost all sympathy. He was not in any way normal.

'You should see mine on a good night,' said the boy in the car. He straightened his jumper.

'Do you want to go?'

Mr O'Donnel reached the car and vented a stream of buff-coloured puke on the bonnet, which was fresh and decorative against the biscuit-brown of the paintwork and the chrome. His meditation on the effect was disturbed by the cognisance that the vehicle was occupied and by intimations of a possible unpleasantness to come. He hinged his torso into the upright and carefully aligned the cuffs of his shirt below the line of his coat-sleeves, a gesture he had admired in his long observation of the British Royal Family, and one he reserved for the petty and the punctilious. His relief on finding the face that peered out from behind the windscreen familiar, mitigated to a great extent the indignation he felt on finding that she was not alone: that uncomfortably close to his daughter was a hairy young skelp. The contrasting paleness of his daughter's countenance, and the bar of shadow that fell from the framework of the car and caressed her mouth, made his throat constrict alarmingly, and the tragedy of generation burst in his chest. This was the entrance to eternity. No sound or movement greeted his thoughts as they took wing, but beneath his hand he could sense the dormant miracle of the internal combustion engine, and above his head stars, that had seen the continents rip, one from the other, wheeled and waited the light years it would take before they could witness his shame. He stood back. The moment cried out for expression. With the flat of his palm, he banged the bonnet of the car.

' "I will tell you.
The barge she sat in, like a burnish'd throne,
Burn'd on the water; the poop was beaten gold,
Purple the snails, and so perfumed, that
The winds were love-sick with them, the oars were
silver
Which to the tune of flutes kept stroke, and made
The water which they beat to follow faster,
As amorous of their strokes. For her own person,
It beggar'd all description . . ." '

*

And so beggar'd, he left the lovers, opened the gate with a creak and entered his house.

Clare came into the kitchen at four o'clock in the morning and found her father sitting at the kitchen table. There was a smell of drink in the room but she couldn't see any bottles. The record player in the living room was left on and the record on the turntable was finished. The sound of the needle going round and round reminded her of the scene in the car and the feeling in her insides.

'Your mother never left, you know. You have her guilty look to perfection.'

She left her father where he was and went into her room where she took down all the posters and started to write on the walls. She wrote all the poems from the school curriculum so that she would be able to study them every night, and so know them off by heart.

'Had I the heaven's embroidered cloths.'

'Golden stockings she had on.'

'I wonder, by my troth, what thou and I
Did, til we loved?'

No more dancing. On the other wall, she copied all her theorems and the basic laws of Physics. Then she lay on the bed and promised herself that she would not sleep for three days and three nights before she closed her eyes and cried.

Mr Snip Snip Snip

The cinema projectionist in Frank's home town was often drunk. When he was thrown out by his wife he slept the night in the projection booth and ate the stale Mars Bars and crisps from the counter in the porch. Once he threw up over a roll of film and had to spend the day cleaning and untangling it. Frank's first experience of 'The Dam Busters' was splattered with small, mucky explosions and the sound-track was a mess.

Even so, everyone went to the pictures, and the boys at the front shouted at the couples snogging in the back row. Frank was not enchanted by the plush red seats, nor by their sexual possibilities, though their smell still sometimes hit him unawares. He felt nothing but the dread of the picture to come, the size of it on the screen, the colours, and the way that it jerked from place to place. The projectionist sometimes put the reels on in the wrong order and the beginning of the picture came halfway through. Most exciting of all was the time that the drunken projectionist fell asleep, and the film, passing close to the bulb, had gone on fire. This was the terror that provoked Frank into a job in television.

*

The air in the editing room had been around the building four times. It seemed to settle there and go cold. Frank sits in a hardback chair in front of the console and a producer sits at his back. What the producer does is his own business. Some of them click their fingers at a cut, or catch their breath or say 'There!' Some of them make faces behind his back, field phone-calls, pace up and down the room. Some of them go away. In front of them are three monitors, and Frank sits all day and staples the picture from one monitor onto the picture of another, without any seams showing. He is the magic of television.

Frank doesn't work on celluloid, he works with tapes that slot in and happen in the machines like they were happening in his head. He can mix or fade, he can freeze the picture at any selected moment, at a laugh, or a fumble. He can make figures move slowly, as if they are pushing their way through honey, or scatter them along the street like Charlie Chaplin. The moment is as long as he likes. Ninety seconds of a finished programme can cover a minute or three years. He is a master of time. No wonder then, that he likes the job.

At three o'clock in the morning the urge to subvert got very strong. He could feed in the word 'FRAUD' behind Charlie Haughey, for a micro-second that would hit the heart of the nation. He could put a dog whistle on the other track, so that all the dogs in the country would bark at the same time. He could slow down an interview the fraction it took to make someone slur like a drunk. Of course he resisted this need, because he was responsible, and part of the broadcasting machine. (Frank's sister beat him up when he was five, for drawing over the walls with her lipstick, and the pain ticked at the edge of his mind when he was very tired, and subversion was at his fingertips.)

Frank sometimes wondered where it all went, the stuff he threw away; smiles, swear-words, faces that slid out of focus. There is a parallel universe, he thought, in 'Star Trek', made up of all the out-takes; the fluffs, blunders and bad (worse) acting that never made it to the final cut. A world where Captain Kirk says 'shit' and Spock's ears become detached. Perhaps the story is better over there. He thought of a universe made up of all the different silences that are nipped, tucked and disposed of. The silence of a hospital at night, the silence when a woman forgets what to say, the silence of a politician. They have to go somewhere. It is a terrible crime, Frank thought, to throw away a silence.

It was the sheer waste that depressed him; the waste of a movement. The woman in the interview raises her arm to smooth an eyebrow and the editor throws away a feast of under-arm hair. He had that gesture, there in his hand, and he threw it away.

When the signal is beamed all the way to Alpha Centauri, the aliens will never see a hairy woman. They will wait for centuries for that one signal, the one they expect and recognise as a call to come and save the world. Who is to say otherwise? Beautiful hairy aliens who never throw anything away except what is deliberately made. Spontaneous Aliens who talk in semaphore and discover everything by accident, in the dustbins of science – which is why they are so advanced.

Frank was dreaming of aliens. He was dreaming of better pay and probably of under-arms. He was dreaming about someone's laugh that he threw out that day. He was dreaming of the split-second where a man wavered and Frank cut him dead.

Over his monitors, Frank had pasted a sign 'The mills of the gods grind slowly, but they grind exceedingly small.'

Soon after he started the job, Frank began to pick up the pictures on the side of the road and string them together in his head. His car stops at the lights beside some road-workers. They talk over the pneumatic drill in glances and a toss of the head. The age of the men is surprising, they have pot bellies and cement dust has settled in the creases of their clothes. Everything is coated with the road; there is cement caked under their fingernails, and their boots are encrusted with tar – in three weeks' time they will be altogether solid. Frank turns the dust, the wheelbarrow full of flaming tar, the traffic cones, and the way the drill turns everything mute, into a beer commercial, where the world is tinted blue. He catches the looks between the men to the rhythm of the song 'Heart of Stone'. It is a good piece, but short. Someone changes the station on a remote control as the traffic lights go green.

It got worse. Frank dreamt of the slice of time between shots, so thin, it couldn't be said to exist at all. He edits and re-edits the film of his father in his sleep. The story of his father is a loose montage that also involves clay and calloused hands, a boot on the side of a spade, a figure moving over the brow of a hill. Sometimes the music is sentimental, sometimes unsettling. Most often he uses the sound of a distant wireless where a quiz show is being played out, and the sound gets closer when his father walks into the room.

The Sunday dinner table is composed of glances from one child to another, and warning looks from his mother. The camera goes under the table, where one small foot in a long grey schoolboy sock kicks out at another. He sees his father's mouth chewing, he sees his knife and fork cutting the meat with delicate violence. The sound-track is silent, except for the scrape of cutlery.

Frank twitches in his sleep. He is running along a mile of tape where his family are caught like ants in amber. Sometimes he feels as though he will fall into the picture, as though the dinner table is under a stretch of water, or glass. Every few seconds he leaps over the gap between one shot and the next, and the gaps become wider.

His father at the table lifts his fork and points it at the camera. Frank leaps away to the salt-cellar, then drives over to his mother's face, jerks back to his father's hand. His father is talking. Frank cuts out the word 'slut' and, before he can stitch it up, falls headlong into the thin, deep hole that he has made. 'You were dreaming.' Moira wakes him with a smile.

Moira makes it easier for him. Every time she moves, she throws it away. She has an abandoned grace. She hardly notices him there on the other side of the table, and he picks up the casual pieces as her hand drops into her lap.

'I don't know.' It is a sigh. She doesn't know that she has spoken. Her hand scratches the top of her leg and Frank drives into work thinking about sex that is entirely random, the way people graze each other in their sleep.

It would be nice to have a child, to go into work after a night of two-hourly feeds and claim it was the pints. It would be nice to say that no matter how frantic the work got, no matter how much the world was cut up into shots and the producer at his back paced the room, there was something of his that had its own slow time. He would do a gardening programme that looked at a rose growing for half an hour, or use a single shot of waves on a beach that went on for as long as the tape was in the camera. No tricks. He would take the memory of his father's cigarette smoke, coming from a hand that had fallen by the side of the chair, and he would stay with it until the cigarette burned down and was dropped on the floor. Force himself to look. Don't cut away.

Moira is hard to find these days. She spends a lot of time in various attitudes around the house. The evening is like a locked-off shot on the sitting room as she fades from the armchair and appears at the table, then fades again and is standing at the window, one hand holding a cigarette at an angle and the other cupped around an elbow that should be wearing evening gloves. When they talk she looks at the carpet as though she sees something growing there. There is a small eddy in her eyes, a slight shift of the current that strays from where she is looking. Moira was always aimless, casual, troubled. It was a look that mothers have and it made his lovemaking hopeful and direct, like a man posting a letter that would change everything.

On Sunday morning Frank surprises himself by getting up early and cleaning the house. He washes the kitchen floor, runs a cloth along the skirting-boards, cleans out the toilet and talks to Moira over the sound of the hoover with a nod of the head. On Monday she wakes up to find him standing by the window with no clothes on, scratching his stomach and staring. He goes to the supermarket on his own and buys some trout and almonds which he makes for her that night, with a salad full of vegetables that he never knew existed until he was twenty-one. He kisses her back while she sleeps and puts his hand over the Y of her legs, to keep her safe.

In unguarded moments while he is at work, Moira flicks into the corner of his eye. There is no pattern to it. She has taken to reading children's books. She has eaten her way through Dr Doolittle and enthuses about Dab Dab the duck.

'What is the difference,' she asks him, 'between doing something and not doing something? When I was a kid, hell would open up if you stepped on the crack in the path and the devil would kiss you – but he never did.'

'You sound disappointed.'

She rubs the corner of her mouth hard with the tip of a finger, as though her lipstick was beginning to smear.

'I want to go somewhere.'

'Anywhere you like.'

'Bolivia?'

'Sure.'

For some reason everyone is using Spanish music in their programmes that week. It makes the cutting very fast and the colours as sharp as an ad for washing powder. He passes a small girl in her communion dress in the street and there are flamenco flounces down the back of her white skirt.

'How about Barcelona? We can afford that.' But she just laughs.

It came together in all the things she threw away. As he sat working at his console, the pictures knitted one into the other. Moira glancing at the phone. Moira rubbing at her thigh, as though there was a burr caught between her leg and her jeans. She comes in through the hall door, with the keys between her teeth and they drop to the floor. She wakes in the morning surprised and her mouth seems caught on the pillow.

It is all in the fraction of the second before he cuts away.

They are sitting in the dining room, in an endless two-shot.

'I love you,' Moira says; she leans over to put her hand on his arm but stops. 'I love you more than anything. Anything. It happened by accident. I don't understand the why. I stepped on the crack in the path by accident and nothing happened. It didn't open up. I didn't fall into hell.'

Reaction shot Frank. The film goes on fire.

'Frank, I can't tell the difference between things. I can't tell the difference between what I want to do, what I mean to do, and something that just happens.'

'What was his name?'

She opens her mouth to speak. He cuts away to the hand that holds the cigarette and before he can stitch it up, falls headlong into the thin, deep hole that he has made.